A SWEETWATER RIVER ROMANCE

WYOMING MOUNTAIN TALES ~ BOOK 3

MISTY M. BELLER

Misty M. Beller
BOOKS

ISBN-13 Trade Paperback: 978-0-9982087-9-4

ISBN-13 Large Print Paperback: 978-1-954810-47-1

ISBN-13 Casebound Hardback: 978-1-954810-48-8

DEDICATION

Blessed be the Lord, who daily loadeth us with benefits, even the God of our salvation.
(Psalms 68:19)

Now the God of hope fill you with all joy and peace in believing,
that ye may abound in hope,
through the power of the Holy Ghost.

Romans 15:13 (KJV)

CHAPTER 1

Advertisement: Seeking a literate person in the western territories willing and eager to correspond with an easterner on a variety of topics. No requirements as to gender, nor the level of education attained, save the ability to read and write in complete sentences and the desire to connect with another human being through the written word. Apply by letter addressed to T.B., Boiling Springs Township, Pennsylvania.

Dear T.B.,

In response to your advertisement seeking a partner in correspondence, I find the idea more than a little intriguing. I do reside in the western territories—Wyoming Territory, to be precise. My gender is male and, having lived at a remote stage coach stop for the past six years, I find myself rather craving the connection afforded only by the application of pen and ink on paper. Curious how much easier it is to organize one's thoughts when writing, isn't it? I wonder if the phenomenon is a response to actually seeing the words take shape before one's eyes? Or perhaps it's the opposite. Not seeing the intended recipient might allow thought to spill out with little inhibition, except the need to organize the words into complete sentences. Although some ignore that requirement altogether, as I have witnessed many times while operating the Western Union Telegraph in our employ. It's a wonder the receiver can obtain any comprehension at all when the message is taxed at five cents per word. But I digress.

In closing, I happily apply for continued correspondence if your interest holds fast. If so, I look forward to your response, at your leisure, of course.

Sincerely,

E. Reid
Rocky Ridge Stage Stop
Wyoming Territory

∽

OCTOBER, 1866
WYOMING TERRITORY

"*L*ooks like it might snow."

Tori Boyd pressed the creases flat in the writing paper as she studied the concise handwriting, a challenging exercise with the sometimes-violent rocking of the stage coach. Such tiny letters, each well-formed, as though its writer had hunched low over the paper, focused on exacting perfection. Not what she would normally prescribe to a man's handwriting.

"See how gray those clouds are? Almost the same color as the river water."

Tori forced her attention up from the stack of letters toward the stage window where her cousin pointed. Yes, the clouds held an ominous feel, as though seizing their breath for what was to come. Yet even the gray pallor they cast on the landscape didn't make it feel dreary. Maybe it was the majesty of the wilderness scene, with the wide expanse of the Sweetwater River traveling beside them. Maybe it was the stirring chill in the air that enlivened her senses.

Maybe it was the fact that she and Opal had left everything they'd known in their quiet Pennsylvania town to venture into this western territory. And now, their very existence could depend on the mercy of the man who'd written the stack of letters in her hands over the past year.

Her gaze wandered back to them. No, her well-being would never again depend on anyone else—especially not a man. Nor would Opal's existence, as long as they both lived. But if Mr. Reid was the kind of man she hoped, he might help them finish the last leg of their dramatic escape.

If he wasn't willing to help them find lodging and procure a decent situation, well, she'd brought them on this endeavor, and it was up to her to see them safely through.

"Do you wish you'd sent word ahead?" Opal's gentle voice broke through Tori's thoughts like a calm trickle of water.

Tori looked up into her cousin's cornflower blue gaze. "Not really. Do you suspect he'll be angry?"

Opal didn't answer, just gave a tight-lipped smile that proclaimed her thoughts on the matter. No change in her opinion since the last time they discussed it.

Maybe it was the fact that Opal was a year older that gave her the aura of wisdom at only nineteen. Or maybe Opal just dealt with life better. Took the bad and looked for the good in it. Her sweet cousin wasn't as brash and reckless as Tori was. A good thing, since Opal's gentle wisdom was the lifeline that had kept them both sane these last ten years.

In their younger days, her resolute calm had kept Tori together through every cruel word spoken by the other children. Kept her from lashing out in a way that would surely have sealed her expulsion from the Boiling Springs School for Girls, despite the ungodly amounts of money Uncle Max poured into the place.

It was Opal who had sheltered Tori in her bed chamber all those nights when her uncle's steward took solace in the brandy and came looking for her. And when kind, brave Opal approached her father with Tori's fears after that first time, the bruise that formed around Opal's eye was enough to start Tori planning retaliation, even in those younger, more innocent days. Only Opal's tearful pleading held her back. But that was the beginning of the bitterness that had crept over her soul. Or perhaps that hadn't been the beginning of bitterness, but it had been the first time she'd welcomed the emotion. It hadn't taken long before she'd clung to it like a shield.

Yet Opal, sweet Opal, stayed gentle and kind. The best of souls.

Which was why Tori couldn't fail Opal now. They were in this together, and she would do whatever it took to keep her cousin safe and happy. And unsullied—a condition that would have been impossible to maintain if they'd stayed back in Boiling Springs.

"Ho!" The driver's voice sounded outside as the coach's steady rocking slowed.

Had they arrived? Fighting down the churning in her stomach, Tori leaned closer to Opal and peered out the small windows.

She glimpsed the corner of a building—unpainted wood siding that seemed newer than many of the ramshackle stage stops they'd visited so far.

Then the coach lurched to a halt, and she was thrown forward, barely catching herself on the opposite seat.

~

*E*zra Reid approached the lathered bay gelding nearest him and rubbed the animal's sweaty neck as he peered up at the stage driver. "I've got the horses if you'll help the passengers. Food's on the table, coffee's on the stove."

"Good." A groan chased Tanner's comment as he hauled himself over the side of the driver's box and down to the ground. "Just two passengers, an' they're both stayin' with you."

Ezra nodded as he reached for the buckles fastening the front horses to the stage. It wasn't often travelers disembarked from their journey at the Rocky Ridge Stage Stop, as remote as this layover was. Not a town within a few hours' ride.

He didn't have time to question the man, though. Had to get these horses unharnessed, make sure everyone was settled inside, and, finally, hitch the new set of four to the coach by the time Tanner was ready to head out. Probably, the driver could handle whatever he and the passengers needed inside, especially since Ezra had laid out everything for a late lunch. But seeing to the passengers was as much his job as caring for the horses.

It had been easier to get it all done when Zechariah was there to help, but his older brother had needed to explore the mountain country and had trusted him with the sole responsibility of the station these next few months.

He'd be tarred and feathered before he'd fail Zeche.

Even in their exhausted condition, the four horses kept him hopping as he led them toward the corral. They must have smelled the snowstorm coming.

"Easy, boy. Settle down. I've got a nice stall for you in time." The bay pinned his ears and snapped his tail at the chestnut giant behind him, and the larger animal retaliated with a squeal. "Quit." Ezra popped the bay's shoulder and tugged them on.

By the time he had the tired horses separated and secured and the fresh teams in harness, he was late heading toward the main house. He'd wait to attach the new animals to the coach when Tanner was ready to leave.

Ezra lengthened his stride across the courtyard between the house and barn. The combination bunkhouse and storeroom spanned one side of the area, which reminded him that he should light the fire in the bunkhouse soon so the place could warm up. The little building hadn't seen visitors in at least a month, but if two men from the stage were disembarking here, they'd probably need somewhere to stay before they began the next leg of their journey.

They'd most likely need to purchase mounts too, since there hadn't been extra horses tied to the rear of the stage. He could take them over to Mara's farm for that. His sister and her husband, Josiah, always seemed to have a string of horses ready for sale on their ranch. Good thing the place was only a half hour's ride away.

Or maybe the passengers had already decided this country was too wild for them and planned to hightail-it back to civilization on the next eastbound stage. They'd still need to stay the night, since Mason wouldn't be coming through with that particular coach 'til mid-morning tomorrow.

Ezra stopped on the stoop of the main house and kicked the mud from his boots. The fire in the bunkhouse would have to wait until he saw the stage off and the horses settled. These Eastern chaps would just have to learn that there was a priority in how work had to be done in the territories. An order to things, if they were to be done right.

Pushing open the door, he shucked his gloves and headed toward the stove. As his eyes adjusted to the dimmer light, he glanced over at the table where three bodies perched around the long wooden planks.

He stopped short as his gaze caught on a shock of red hair. No, not a shock. Thick, springy curls pulled loose from their owner's attempt to restrain them at the base of her neck.

Her neck. His guests must be a man and wife then, heading toward a new life in the western territories. He shifted his gaze from the woman to take in the measure of her husband, but his focus almost skittered past the thin blond woman sitting beside the first.

Two women? What in blazes?

His focus pulled back to the fire-haired lady, just to be sure his mind hadn't deceived him. And that was the exact moment she looked up at him.

Their eyes met and something caught him up short. Maybe it was the intensity of her gaze. And then, as quickly as they captured him, her penetrating eyes released him, and she looked away.

He took the opportunity to turn back to the stove, gripping the wooden handle of the oven door as he struggled to gather his wits. Hadn't Tanner said he only had two passengers and they would both be disembarking the stage at the Rocky Ridge? Surely these women weren't his guests. They couldn't be traveling alone.

He shifted to grab the coffee pot and scoot it toward a cooler part of the stove, which gave him an opportunity to glimpse the women from the corner of his eye. His peripheral vision was blurry, but he could make out the image of that carrot-colored hair. Or...maybe not carrot exactly. A bit darker, but still striking.

Pulling his focus back in front of him, he leaned down to toss a few more chunks of wood into the firebox. Where was he going to put these women, if they did indeed need lodging? Surely they'd need a place, at least for tonight. They must be turning back to ride the east-bound stage tomorrow like so many others before them. Going back to a more civilized land after the west turned out even wilder than they'd anticipated. From that quick glance, they seemed to be respectably dressed—maybe even part of the wealthier set, although he couldn't be sure.

The bunkhouse wouldn't do, with its two old straw ticks barely propped up off the floor. At least he and Zeche had added a wood floor in the building instead of leaving it as packed dirt, although that was more to keep the rodents out of the supplies than to accommodate their few guests. But such a rustic, dirty structure was hardly fit for two ladies.

And they couldn't stay in the house with him, an unmarried man. Although maybe he could sleep in the bunkhouse...

But...that felt wrong. Maybe he'd been alone in this wilderness long enough to lose proper judgement, but this wasn't any place for a pair of ladies—unchaperoned and unprotected.

After scooping up the leather pad to protect his hand, he grasped the handle on the coffee pot and turned to face his guests. He tried to keep his gaze casual as he took in the two women sitting beside each other, opposite Miles Tanner. The red-haired lady drew his focus like a homing beacon, but he didn't allow himself to stare, just stepped forward and refilled the tin cups with coffee. "Y'all made it in just before the snow."

"Yep. Hoping I can get all the way to South Pass City before it hits." Tanner took an audible gulp from his mug, then clanged the metal onto the table. "Reckon' I'm gonna head out. You gals sure you wanna stay on?"

Ezra raised his focus to the women. "Where are you headed?"

The blond lady looked uncertain, darting a glance at her friend. The other raised a strong chin and met his gaze. Squarely. With more pluck than he often saw in stage travelers—male or female. Usually, the wilderness they'd traveled to reach this spot was enough to take the starch out of all adventurous spirits. But apparently not this lady.

"Actually, we'd like to stay in this area." Her voice rang strong and clear. She glanced at her friend, but not in the hesitant way the other gal had. The look seemed to be more encouragement than anything else. "Opal and I would like to settle here. Maybe start a bakery, if there's sufficient clientele. Or if not, we'll find other suitable situations."

He couldn't help but raise his brows at her. "A bakery? Here?" The question slipped out before he could grab it. But *really*. She apparently thought this area a great deal more civilized than it was.

Ezra shot a glance at Tanner, who met his look with brows lowered in a way that mirrored his own feelings. Half incredulity, half concern. Ezra cleared his throat. "Ma'am. I'm not sure we have enough people in the towns of South Pass and Atlantic City combined to support a bakery. Most people in this area are miners or ranchers. The more civilized men have wives and children, but they're spread out several hours apart. The rest tend to be rough around the edges."

Her petite nose flared in a way that reminded him of a peeved mother hen guarding her brood, so he eased the intensity of his tone. "You might do better at one of the towns farther east. St. Louis maybe or even Independence."

The ruffled collar at her neck shifted as she seemed to take in a deep breath and let it out. Another moment passed before she spoke.

"Thank you for that advice, Mr. Reid, but I think we'd rather look here." She paused, like she was holding her breath.

It was two whole beats of his pulse before the last of her words sank in. How did she know his name? Tanner must have told her. He shot another look at the man, but the driver seemed to be studying the ladies with a scowl.

"You are Mr. Reid, aren't you?" The lady's voice pulled Ezra's focus again, and something about the way she watched him, intensity emanating from her gaze, made his stomach tighten.

"Ye—es." He drew the word out, letting his tone imply his uneasy question. What was she getting at?

"I'm Tori Boyd. I believe we've…met."

Silence filtered through the room as her words slowly penetrated his thick skull. Tori…Boyd? As in T. Boyd from Boiling Springs, Pennsylvania? His correspondence partner? His mind wouldn't stop spinning, yet it seemed unable to form a coherent thought.

CHAPTER 2

"*D*o you remember me?" The hesitation in Miss Boyd's voice finally broke through the questions whirling in Ezra's brain.

He forced his slack jaw to close, then cleared his throat. "I...yeah." Narrowing his gaze, he took in the length of her. She was prettier than he'd ever thought as he wrote those silly letters. When he'd first seen that advertisement in the Eastern paper, he'd thought it was unusual for someone to want a writing partner just for the sake of sending letters, but he hadn't questioned it too deeply. She'd made it sound like she wanted to hear fascinating stories about life in the west. So, he'd responded, starting up a regular correspondence that never failed to be interesting as the months progressed. And he'd not had to embellish much on his stories of life at this stage coach stop in the Wyoming Territory. Between the wild animals and even wilder men, it seemed there was always some new excitement to describe, whether it came on the stage or galloped into the yard from a different means.

But he'd never expected *her* to show up on his doorstep.

"Mr. Reid. Perhaps I could have a word with you outside?" Her voice came strong and full, like she wasn't afraid to speak her opinion.

Yet there was something beautiful about the sound, like fine china. Maybe it was her polished accent. Certainly more cultured than the few frontier women who lived in South Pass City. Of course, that was to be expected since she was from the east.

"I suppose." Curiosity niggled in his chest as he followed her swishing skirts out the door and down the step to the brown grass beside the house.

She scanned the little courtyard, apparently taking in the bunkhouse and the larger barn beside it. All the buildings had been rebuilt a couple years ago after a Cheyenne war party burned the original structures to the ground. The improvements they'd added had been minor, but helpful. But how rustic did the place look through her eyes?

She seemed to raise her gaze to the trees beyond, and the bluffs that rose above the juniper and pines. "It's pretty, this land. Just like you described." Her voice had softened, as though she were lost in a memory.

He couldn't help but study her as the afternoon glow outlined her profile. She was a pretty thing, with refined features and vibrant hair. It wasn't so much the red of it that stole his breath, although the color had first captured his eye. The loose curls seemed to make the locks spring to life. He fought the urge to step forward and slip his fingers through its thickness.

She turned to face him then, stilling the impulse and snapping him back to reality. "I bet you're wondering why I'm here?"

He raised his brows. "A little." She seemed to want to take the reins of this conversation. She could drive for now. At least until he wrapped his mind around exactly where they were headed.

"Due to an unexpected circumstance, my cousin and I decided it was time to leave our little town in Pennsylvania. You made this country sound so inviting, we thought it would be a nice place to settle." She motioned around, as though the cluster of buildings and winter grass were as good as a Boston pleasure ground.

The inkling in his gut that usually warned him when something wasn't quite right now tightened into a solid knowing. Not only was she simple-minded if she thought she and that other woman could live out here alone, but there was something about her overly casual tone that sounded like she'd carefully prepared and memorized her little speech.

Which meant she was probably running from something.

Was one of them in the family way? Escaping a soiled reputation? He'd be hard-pressed to think of another reason why two genteel women would leave the town where they'd been raised to head out west on their own. But if they thought they could easily fend for themselves—and care for a newborn child in the process—they were delusional.

He eyed Miss Boyd. This first introduction didn't make her seem very logical, but the letters she'd sent had seemed so grounded, in a spunky sort of way. He knew little about her and nothing about her cousin. After all, a woman could put any fabrication she wanted on paper and he'd be none the wiser. And now she'd shown up on his doorstep, and he had to figure out the truth.

"You're familiar with the area. Where do you think is the best place for us to begin our search for work?" Her voice prodded, a little less forceful than before.

He met her gaze. "I can't think of a place within a week's ride. You'd do best to wait for tomorrow's eastbound stage and head back to Boiling Springs." His comment might be rude, but he couldn't quite squelch the frustration springing from her recklessness.

She stiffened, and the friendliness in her expression ebbed as she raised her chin. Fire flashed in those brown eyes. "We're not going back, Mr. Reid. If you'd rather not help us, that's fine. But we'll make our way to a new life."

Guilt pressed hard on his chest. Whatever had driven them into this crazy scheme must have been extreme, and it wasn't his job to make her feel worse about her past. He'd be hamstrung and quartered before he'd let these two women wander from town to town on their own, looking for a *situation*. They'd find a situation all right, whether they wanted that particular type or not. Probably ten times worse than anything they'd have found in the little hamlet of Boiling Springs.

He straightened and eased out a sigh. "I'll help. Let me see the stage off, then we'll get you both settled."

The stubborn jut of her chin eased into a soft smile, and the way it blossomed over her face made something flip in his gut.

~

He'd agreed to help. Tori leaned against the cabin's open door, biting back a grin as she watched activity around the stage. Mr. Reid worked steadily with the horses, hitching the team of four to the coach while Mr. Tanner hauled their luggage into the house.

She should be doing something besides standing there ogling Mr. Reid.

The clang of tinware from the kitchen grabbed her attention, and she turned to see Opal stacking used plates at the table. Yes, that was the place to help. She stepped into motion, filling a large kettle with what looked to be clean water from a nearby bucket, scrapping a bit of lye soap into the liquid, and setting it on the stove to heat. She and Opal worked in easy silence, cleaning the remains of their meal and the dishes Mr. Reid had employed to prepare the food, along with what seemed to be the plates and forks he'd used for the past several meals.

The kitchen wasn't dirty per se, but it was clear the place hadn't seen a woman's touch in a while.

When Mr. Tanner came to take his leave, they both paused to offer their heartfelt thanks. She'd felt safe in his care since he'd taken over the coach that morning, but her relief at his apparent competence and integrity was nothing compared to the feeling of finally reaching the Rocky Ridge Station.

She and Opal were safe now. Mr. Reid could direct them to the best place for them to start new lives in this beautiful land.

Opal was straightening the dishes on the shelf into neat stacks and rows while Tori folded the hand towel at the washbasin.

A boot thud sounded outside and the door pushed open.

Tori turned to face the man as he stepped inside and hung his hat on a peg by the wall.

He was silent while he shucked his gloves and his gaze scanned the room, catching on her. His fingers worked each of the half-dozen buttons down his coat. There was a curiosity in his look as he seemed to appraise her, then Opal, who had halted her work to watch him.

Her cousin came alive when his attention landed on her, and she took quick steps forward, extending her hand as she moved. "I don't think we've officially met, Mr. Reid. I'm Opal Boyd, her cousin." She motioned toward Tori.

He looked at her extended hand as though it were a curiosity, then up at her face. He cautiously took just her fingers like he wasn't sure whether he should clasp and shake or bow and kiss them. Tori nibbled the inside of her lip against a grin. This was the Opal that hadn't appeared since before Tori had left their home on her eighteenth birthday. It was good to see a little spunk back in her manner.

"It's a pleasure, Miss Boyd." He half-bowed over her fingers, seeming to recover from his surprise. Then he withdrew his hand from Opal's and strode to the shelf where she'd been straightening dishes. He pulled down the three tin mugs they'd just washed and stacked. Then he moved to the coffee pot and poured brew into all three. "Come sit and we'll talk." Turning his back to them, he strode toward the table.

Apparently, he had no doubt they'd jump at his command. For half a second, Tori was tempted to disregard him and take up the broom in the corner. But that was no way to treat a man who she hoped would help them. And she wasn't ready to test his temper.

She followed Opal to the table, and they took the same places they'd occupied before, with Mr. Reid facing them across the wooden surface.

He sipped his coffee while he studied them, a thoughtful expression forming a valley between his brows. He was more handsome than she'd let herself imagine when she read his letters. She'd tried to keep a realistic perspective, thinking of him as a buck-tooth, balding, middle-aged man who liked to spit tobacco. But Mr. Reid was nothing of the kind, with the strong, perfectly-proportioned angles of his face and the way his shoulders filled out the gray wool of his shirt.

What did he think as he perused over the rim of his mug? She wasn't sure she wanted to know. And she definitely didn't like this feeling that their fate somehow rested in his hands, no matter how much her instincts told her they could trust him.

She needed to get control of the conversation. She slipped both hands around the warm metal of her cup and gave him what she hoped was a competent look. "I suppose we'll be needing to rent horses from you, if you have any to spare. Perhaps you could give us a list of people we might speak with in the surrounding towns?"

He raised his brows. "I was just thinking about that." He placed his cup on the table and straightened. "I think for tonight, I'm going to take you over to my sister's ranch. She and her husband own a spread about half an hour from here across the river. It'll be a good safe place for you both until we figure out your next steps."

Tori's heart leapt as she absorbed his words. "Do you think your sister would be interested in hiring a cook and housekeeper? We'd like to stay together if possible, but I think we would settle for neighboring ranches if I could find another place nearby." Tori shot a glance at Opal. Her cousin bobbed her chin, a glimmer of hope shimmering in her pale blue eyes.

"I...um...don't know about that." He cleared his throat. "I was thinking more that they could provide a safe place for you to live until we make other arrangements. I'm not sure she and Josiah are ready to hire on help."

The hope burgeoning in Tori's chest evaporated. "Oh. All right. We can pay her for board." She really didn't want charity from this man's sister.

Mr. Reid opened his mouth to respond, but a clacking sound from the corner grabbed his attention. He padded quietly toward the corner where the sound emanated.

The telegraph.

He'd written about the entertaining messages he passed along the line, but she'd forgotten about it. Now he scribbled furiously on a sheet of paper as the clicking continued.

She couldn't help but watch, mesmerized, as he wrote for another minute. She studied the jumble of metal and wires comprising the machine on the desk. Connected lines ran up the wall to the roof, where they must feed through a hole to the outside, although she couldn't see evidence of daylight leaking through. The opening had been plugged well.

At last, the noise ceased, and a moment later, Mr. Reid straightened. He let out a breath and looked around, as though just now returning to his surroundings. His gaze met Tori's and stalled there. "I just need to send this message. Sorry for the interruption."

"Of course." She pushed to her feet before her brain could catch up with her body. "Can I watch?"

He shrugged as she approached, then turned back to the desk and pulled out the chair tucked underneath it. After settling in front of the machine, he started sending the message. His finger tapped out the clicks almost faster than her mind could register them, but she narrowed her focus to the sounds, trying to differentiate between the long clicks for the dashes and the short clicks for the dots.

She'd read enough about telegraphs in the newspapers to understand the theory behind the communication, and she'd watched the telegrapher at work when she'd had business in Boiling Springs's combination postal and telegraph office. But she'd never been quite this close.

As she focused on the sounds and the movement of Mr. Reid's finger, the long and short beats gradually began to distinguish themselves. But it was nothing short of fantastic that he could think quickly enough to transmit the scribbled message into codes for each letter.

At last, his finger stilled, and when he straightened, Tori realized how close she was hovering over him. She stepped back, almost tripping over her skirts. And when he rose and pushed the chair back under the desk, he seemed to tower over her short frame. Of course, most people towered over her. She steeled herself not to show her intimidation, but it didn't require as much effort as usual to keep a calm façade. He didn't ruffle her defenses as much as most men she met. Didn't trigger the spurt of fear that made her feel the need to retaliate. No, something about Mr. Reid's presence made her feel protected.

And that feeling alone was enough to terrify.

CHAPTER 3

a question slipped into Tori's mind and spilled out before she could tether it. "What's your given name, Mr. Reid?" She tilted her head and affected a casual look, which would hopefully make the question seem less intrusive. He'd used the initial *E* in his letters, but he didn't seem like an Edward or Elijah.

He raised his brows. "Ezra. What's yours?"

Cheeky thing, he was. She bit back a smile. "Victoria." His brows rose even higher at the stuffy name she despised. "But I allow friends to call me Tori."

The corner of his mouth twitched. "And what shall I call you?"

Why had she started this ridiculous line of conversation? One of these days she'd learn to filter her words. Should she let him call her by her given name? It was a liberty, and she wasn't in the habit of allowing favors to men. Not at all. That gender tended to take their own freedoms whether she handed them over or not.

Yet she'd come all this way because she was fairly sure she could trust Ezra Reid, and maybe it was time to test him. "You may call me Tori." And in an effort to keep some semblance of control of the conversation, she turned and strode back to take her place at the table. "Shall we finish discussing our plan to find suitable work?"

Several beats of her pulse pounded in her neck before Ezra's boots thumped across the room to join them. He sank into his chair and leaned forward to rest his elbows on the table, clasping his hands in front of him. They were strong hands that seemed capable of anything asked of them. Yet quick and sensitive enough to tap out a message almost faster than her brain could process it.

She leaned forward and met Ezra's gaze. "Could you teach me how to send messages on the telegraph?"

He pulled back, his chin lowering as his brows rose again. Then his face relaxed as a warm chuckle slipped out. "I can't seem to predict what's going to pop out of your mouth."

"That's the case for all of us." Opal's soft voice held a mirth that matched his.

Tori fought the burn rising into her cheeks. She wasn't always this impulsive. It must be nerves from their unsettled future. She shot Opal a glare, to which her cousin responded with a cheeky grin, the little minx.

Perhaps it was best they got back to their earlier topic. She turned to Ezra. "I'll agree to board with your sister until we can make other arrangements. But my other questions still remain. Do you have horses we can rent until we procure jobs? I imagine we'll need sturdy transportation to travel the area."

His gaze narrowed on her as if he were trying to read something in her expression. "Is there anyone we need to worry about? Someone who might not be pleased you left Boiling Springs?"

An image of Jackson flitted through her mind, his bushy black brows lowered in a way that he seemed to think made him desirable. Her gut roiled, but she pushed the picture out of her mind. Her uncle's steward wouldn't travel thousands of miles to find her or Opal. Now that they were gone, the lazy man would simply turn his attentions to another female on the Riverdale estate. She swallowed past a lump. She couldn't worry about any of the others. Opal was safe—at least for now—and it might take all her focus to make sure she stayed that way.

She raised her chin a notch and met Ezra's gaze. "No one." The thought of her uncle—Opal's father—sent a twinge through her.

Uncle Max could very well be searching for them. Maybe. He hadn't seemed concerned about their peace of mind or safety while she and Opal had lived under his roof, but he was just selfish enough to chase them when they disappeared. They hadn't left any clues about where they'd gone, so there was no way he would find them. Of that, she was certain. Fairly certain.

Ezra studied her for a long moment, and something about the intensity in his gaze—or maybe it was the earnestness—made her want to give in and pour their whole sordid story out before him.

But she couldn't do that. Not only did she have to stay strong for Opal's sake, but she couldn't ever tell the things that had transpired. It was all too…staining.

So she tightened her jaw against his look.

Another moment passed, and his expression softened. He shifted his gaze to Opal. "Can you think of anyone who might be searching for you, Miss Opal?"

Tori's stomach tightened again, and she held her breath, willing her cousin to be strong. Opal blanched a little, but maybe the loss of color wouldn't be noticeable to someone not well acquainted with her. She shook her head. "I don't think so."

Poor Opal. The thought that her father would allow what Jackson had planned must be devastating, and a fresh spurt of anger flared through Tori's veins.

"All right, then."

Tori turned back to Ezra as he pushed up from the table.

"I'll go hitch the wagon, and we'll head to Mara's."

~

*E*zra's thoughts jumbled as he buckled the harnesses around Jim and Jack, the more laid-back pair of stage horses he liked to use with the farm wagon. Something wasn't right with his two guests. His first instinct had been to assume they'd lost their good sense on a hair-brained scheme, but as he'd watched and listened to what they said and the answers they hedged around, deeper suspicions began to clog his throat.

The shimmer of fear on Miss Opal's face had been nothing compared to the deep-seated pain he'd glimpsed in the depths of Tori's wide brown eyes. She'd concealed the emotion quickly enough, masking it with that stubborn jut of her chin. But if her fear ran that deep, it helped make sense of why two young women would abandon their home and everything they knew to come west on what seemed like a whim.

And they'd come to him.

He still couldn't wrap his mind around what he'd written in his letters that had made him and this wild territory seem like the safest place to be, but they'd come for help. And he'd do every last thing in his power to see them settled, safe and comfortable.

~

Tori studied the familiar scenery from the wagon bench as they rode. For about a quarter of an hour now, the view had seemed to be the same road she and Opal had just traversed on the stage. Maybe she should ask Ezra if he planned to take them back east himself.

Not that she really thought he'd do that, but at least he would see that she recognized the terrain. She'd learned long ago not to let men think she was a helpless creature. The more competent they considered a woman, the less they thought of her an easy target. Of course, any fourteen-year-old girl would be naïve. Experience could be a swift teacher, though, as swift as innocence could fade. At least that had been the case for her.

She pulled herself out of the bitter memories as Ezra turned off the main road—if you could call it a road. It was really a set of tracks grooved into the frozen ground. He reined the horses around a stand of barren tree trunks that would likely leaf into a vibrant forest in the spring.

"How far to your sister's place?" She pulled her cloak tighter around herself as a gust of wind flipped up the edges. On her right, Opal snuggled in closer. Tori had taken the center position on the seat —sort of a buffer between Opal and the man—but that left her cousin more exposed to the weather. She wrapped an arm around her to share their body warmth.

"Not much farther. We have to drive up here to the low water crossing for the wagon. It's a little quicker ride on horseback because of the shortcut, but still not too far this way."

"We could have ridden the horses." As the words slipped from her mouth, she heard the defensiveness in her tone. "I mean, you don't have to make special concessions for us. Opal and I are both capable in the saddle."

"I'm sure you'll have use for those skills out here." Ezra's tone stayed even and genial. "I thought it'd be easier to transport your trunk and bags with the wagon, though."

Right. She sank back against the seat. She would have realized that too if she'd thought before speaking.

The river soon came into view through the tree skeletons. And as they neared the water, the last of the obstructions cleared and a pretty farmhouse came into view across the way. Although the wooden siding wasn't painted, the porch spanning the front and the rock chimney climbing the left side gave the place a pleasant, homey air.

The horses splashed into the water, and the wagon groaned as it teetered down the gradual slope to the river. Thankfully, the tributary seemed only a couple feet deep in this section. Low water crossing, indeed.

As they lurched up the opposite bank, Tori clutched Opal's arm with one hand, and the edge of the seat with her other, but soon the ground leveled and the wagon returned to its steady rocking rhythm.

A noise sounded from the house ahead, although they were still over a hundred feet away.

"Uncle Ezra!" A child's voice called before Tori made sense of the movement on the porch, then a figure clad in brown ran through the winter grass.

Ezra slapped the reins on the horses' backs to urge them on, then pulled the leathers tight a minute later as the child reached the wagon. The girl clambered up, all arms and legs and blond hair barely restrained by her braid.

"Uncle Ezra. What are you doing here?" She climbed right into his lap, and Tori slid closer to Opal to give space for the squirming child. The girl gripped the reins in front of Ezra's hands and jiggled the leathers. "G'dup, Jim. G'dup, Jack."

Ezra chuckled, letting her take over as if she knew her place exactly. He removed one of his hands from the reins to grip his niece around the waist. "How are you, Katie? You keeping your momma out of trouble today?"

The girl turned to look at him and wrinkled her lightly-freckled nose. "Momma never gets into trouble."

Ezra tapped that nose. "She's got the wool pulled over your eyes, I see."

Katie rolled her blue gaze as she turned back to the horses, and Tori couldn't help but chuckle at the look that reminded her so much of herself at that age. Give the girl red hair and brown eyes, and they could be twins.

Of course, that was back in the happy times. Before her parents went to prison, abandoning her to the care of her uncle's household. Before everything else.

"Katie, I'd like you to meet some friends of mine." Ezra's steady voice broke through the memories. "This is Miss Tori and Miss Opal."

"How'do, ma'am. Ma'am." She dipped her chin to each of them in turn, shyness seeming to overcome her boldness from a second before.

Tori glanced at Ezra and was captured by the glimmer of pride on his face as he watched his niece. So much caring shone there. Could it possibly be real? Not in her experience with men, but maybe Ezra was different.

"Ezra?" A woman's voice pulled their attention, and Tori turned to see a pretty lady approach with a hand raised to shade her eyes. As she neared and lowered her hand, her features came clear. Large brown eyes seemed to illuminate her face, and her brown hair hung in a braid as Katie's did. Her complexion was darker than her daughter's, so Katie's father must be fair-haired and blue-eyed.

Ezra positioned his hands over the girl's on the reins and pulled the horses to a stop with a "whoa." Then he slipped out from under his niece and climbed down the side of the wagon. The girl scrambled behind him, and he fit his hands around her willowy waist to swing her to the ground.

His gaze swung up to Tori's, but he raised a finger. "I'll be right back." The twinkle in his eyes softened them in a way that called to her.

Then he turned away and met the woman—apparently, his sister, Mara. He gripped her elbows and leaned down to plant a kiss on her cheek. Then he straightened and held her at arms' length.

She couldn't hear the words he murmured in his deep tenor, but the affection in his actions—and the way his sister reached up to pat his cheek—brought a sting to Tori's eyes. She forced herself to look away before the burn broke through her barriers.

Instead, she turned and focused on Opal, giving her a hopeful smile. "We're here."

Opal returned a knowing look and reached for her gloved hand, offering a little squeeze. "We're here."

Ezra turned back to them, leaving his sister's side to approach the wagon. Tori didn't usually allow men to help her from carriages and wagons, but she accepted the hand he offered, keeping her gaze on the wagon instead of meeting his.

"Ladies, I'd like you to meet my sister, Mara English. Mara, this is Miss Tori Boyd…" he paused as Tori reached the ground and released his hand. "…and Miss Opal Boyd."

Tori brushed her gloves together, then stepped forward to greet Mrs. English.

She hadn't offered more than a smile, though, before Ezra spoke again. "Mara, these ladies will be your houseguests for a few days. Shall I put their things in the spare room?"

A burn swept into Tori's face at his bold declaration, not even asking if their presence would be acceptable.

"If that's all right with you and Mr. English." Opal, always the thoughtful one, jumped in to soften feelings.

"We'll pay you for the lodging, of course," Tori added. She didn't plan to be the object of the family's charity. She and Opal had a little bit of savings left after the train and stage fares. But they would need to find jobs soon.

"I'm so happy to have you." Mrs. English sent them a smile, but it seemed a little wobbly. Was she just being polite? But her complexion had gone pale, too, and her lips a vibrant red. She looked almost ill.

Tori had the urge to step forward and take her arm in case the woman collapsed, but before she could act, Mrs. English whirled and started toward the house.

"Please come in and make yourselves at home. I need to check something." She broke into a jog, one hand raising her skirts and the other pressed to her bodice.

Tori glanced at Opal, whose worried look showed the same concerns that tightened Tori's middle. But Ezra hadn't seemed to notice anything unusual. He was handing their bags down to Katie, who clutched a carpet bag in each hand and was trying to fit a third under her arm. The waif was practically buried under the things.

Tori strode to her and took two of the satchels, handing Opal's to her.

"Just set those on the porch and I'll carry them in with this trunk." Ezra lowered the chest to the ground as though it were made of willows. "As soon as I settle the horses."

"I'll come help with Jim and Jack," Katie called.

Tori took the bag from her, then Ezra's niece scampered to the horses' heads.

He jumped to the ground and sent Tori a wry look before he strode off to join the girl, who was now prodding the horses forward.

Tori couldn't help but watch them go, taking in the sight of the tall man and the child in the waning light of dusk. From all appearances, Ezra was a better man than she'd even allowed herself to hope.

Yet that might prove to be a challenge of its own. Despite how easy it would be to trust him, she couldn't give over the responsibility for Opal's safety to any man.

Not even Ezra Reid.

CHAPTER 4

The quiet tap of the barn door closing was almost swallowed by Katie's chatter, but Ezra didn't have to look up from brushing Jim to know it was his sister who had entered. The only other person it could be was Josiah, but little Katie had already told him her Papa was out tending the fence line. Besides, his brother-in-law wouldn't slip into the barn the way Mara did. She was probably studying him until she could read the answers she wanted from his look. Maybe she'd go away without giving voice to her questions.

Mara padded toward them, the skirt of her brown dress swishing over the hay-strewn floor. "Katherine, it's time to wash up for dinner, then please set the table. Six places." Mara's voice was so soft yet seemed to hold a strength that not even his niece would buck against.

The girl did issue a dramatic sigh, though, and flung her arms around the bay gelding she'd been brushing. "Goodbye, Jack. I'll see you again someday."

Ezra bit back a chuckle. Wherever had his niece learned such dramatics?

When Katie finally trounced out of the barn and shut the door behind her, he turned back to brushing the horse. These two geldings were brothers, a year apart and almost a matched pair. Jim, the elder and a slightly darker bay, had the benefit of age to mellow him more than his sibling.

"Anything you want to tell me?"

He knew exactly how Mara would look without turning to glance at her. Feet planted, slightly spread. Both hands on her hips. Stubborn jut to her chin. Always the protective big sister, or more aptly, momma hen.

Their own mother had died when he was so young, he wasn't sure whether the few memories he held onto were real or only recreations from the stories Pa had told.

But Mara had always been with him, and he had the feeling he wouldn't shake her protectiveness even if he lived to be a hundred and ten. And now she waited for him to say something. His sister wouldn't give up until she thought she knew everything, so he might as well give her some meat to chew on.

"The Miss Boyds came on today's westbound stage. They're looking for work in this area, and need a safe place to stay until they find something." He met her gaze with a frank expression. "I didn't think it proper for them to sleep at the stage stop with only me there, so I hoped you wouldn't mind putting them up for a while."

Her expression softened into that caring look he'd known would come. "Of course. They can stay as long as they need to. But where in the land of Goshen do they think they'll find work? There's nothing around here for unattached women, unless…" Red splotches touched her cheeks, glaring against the pallor the lantern light had cast on her face. Although, as he looked closer, he wondered if maybe her pale skin was caused by more than just the glow of light. Was she ill?

"Ezra, they're not…*that* kind of women, are they?"

He had to blink to refocus his thoughts onto her meaning, but the moment her words registered, heat crawled up his own neck. "No. No, of course not. I mean…" Did he really know for sure? But he was fairly certain. He met Mara's gaze. "They're not like that. Tori said they'd like to open a bakery, but I don't think there's any chance the area could support a specialty business like she means. I was hoping to find them work at a hotel or boarding house somewhere."

Her pert brows rose. *"You're going to find them work?"*

He pinched his lips. Was he? He hadn't really thought that far into his plans. But the two women couldn't very well traipse about the countryside asking for a *situation*. No telling how many times they'd be accosted. He shrugged. "Maybe. We'll see."

Mara narrowed her eyes and studied him. "Just how well do you know these women? And how long?"

And this was exactly why he should have known better than to bring them to his bossy sister.

But the barn door opened then, bringing a gust of wind and a blessed break from the inquisition as Josiah stepped inside. He led a tired chestnut horse, and his expression matched the animal's until his gaze landed on Mara and Ezra. His steps veered toward his wife. He slipped his arm around her waist and planting a less-than-chaste kiss on her cheek.

A smile brushed her face even as her gaze skittered to Ezra. She leaned back to study her husband's expression, and the look was so tender, Ezra had to turn away. He shouldn't be here, invading this private moment.

"Good to see you, Ezra." Josiah's voice called his attention back, and Ezra nodded at the man from across Jim's back.

He stepped around the animal and reached to clasp Josiah's hand, then took the reins of his weary horse. "You look worn out. I'll settle this fella while you head inside. I brought houseguests, but I hope that won't be a problem."

Josiah's weary brows raised as he looked between Ezra and Mara. "Houseguests?"

Mara slipped her hands around his waist in a way that made it look like she were helping support him. "Two ladies that came on the stage today. They're going to stay with us until they find work in the area. Is that all right?" She said it so sweetly, as though Josiah had the final say on the matter.

But Ezra knew well enough the man wouldn't go against Mara's wants unless he foresaw danger. Besides, his brother-in-law's heart was almost as big as Mara's when it came to taking in strays.

"Sure." He shrugged, and Mara turned him toward the door.

"Come in soon, Ezra." She called over her shoulder. "We'll hold dinner for you."

When the barn door closed again, the peace that settled over the place held an appeal that almost made him dawdle as he secured the animals in stalls. But he had two guests waiting for him inside—and a lot of details to work out.

And he couldn't deny a strange curiosity to see a certain redhead again. Maybe he'd be able to figure her out if he spent a little more time with her.

~

*A*s they all settled around the long table, Tori kept her hands in her lap until she could take stock of the landscape. Meals in the Riverdale dining hall had been silent, sometimes daunting affairs, and she'd had the back of her hand caned more than once as a girl for grabbing at food before it was offered her. Yet the canings issued by his butler were sometimes preferable to the icy glares and silent treatment Uncle Max dished out.

Yet here in the English family's home, the atmosphere had relaxed into an easy camaraderie. Mr. English greeted them with a pleasant courtesy, although he didn't spare many words. Katie had shown her and Opal which seats would be theirs, side-by-side on one of the long ends, across from Mrs. English and Katie. That left the two men as bookends, with Ezra positioned nearest her.

Now, as chairs scraped into place, she looked to Mr. English to take his helping first. Instead, the man bowed his head so that only the crown of his dark hair stared back at her. A glance around the table showed the others did the same, and with a flash, she realized what was happening.

A prayer.

She'd known some people, including a few school mates through the years, who'd kept the custom before meals. But she'd never been well-enough acquainted with any of them to ask why they did it or what they said.

Now, she glanced at Opal, who slipped her hand into Tori's as she bowed her head. She squeezed Opal's grip to offer reassurance. As long as they were together, nothing should unnerve them.

And then Tori's gaze caught on something else. Opal's hand in Mr. English's. A flush crept up her neck for her cousin's sake, but as she darted a glance at Mrs. English, she saw the woman's hand was clasped her husband's other.

The man started to speak his prayer aloud while Tori struggled to make sense of what she was seeing.

And then something tapped her arm, and she almost jumped. Ezra looked at her through a slit in the corner of his eyes. His hand lay on the table, palm up, and he wiggled his fingers in a strange motion.

She sent him a look that hopefully expressed her lack of understanding. But even she knew her head should be bowed with eyes closed as Mr. English continued his prayer.

Your hand. He mouthed the words clearly enough for comprehension to dawn over her like a cold rain shower.

She darted another glance around the table, confirming that every other person linked hands with those on either side. This custom she'd never seen before, but that wasn't surprising. She'd been so little exposed to religion. Uncle Max had forbidden it at Riverdale.

With a reluctance stronger than the situation should require, she laid her palm atop his on the smooth plank of the table. He closed his warm fingers around hers, swallowing her small hand in his strength. The warmth of him slid up her arm to a sheltered place in her heart, filling it with a sense of security she should guard against. She and Opal weren't safe. Not yet. And a man should be the last person to ever make her feel so.

Mr. English soon finished his prayer with an "amen," and it might have been her imagination, but it felt like Ezra gave her hand a gentle squeeze before he released it.

She withdrew her arm, careful to keep her gaze away from his.

"You have to try some of my sister's sourdough bread." His voice came out so genially, as though he hadn't just held her hand in a connection from which her skin still tingled.

"I'm getting almost as good as Josiah with the bread." Mara sent her husband a look that could only be called adoring, brightening her pale face.

"Better." The man glanced down at the beans he ladled onto his plate with a chuckle, almost as though trying to deflect the compliment.

Mrs. English turned to Tori and Opal with a smile. "My husband was once a chef in a fine eastern hotel."

A chef? She glanced at their host again, trying to picture the man with an apron and flour smeared across his chin. He had a strong face with startling blue eyes and hair cut fairly short, although it curled around the ends where sweat and dirt had dried. The impression of his hat remained as a low crown.

His gaze flickered between her and Opal, and his skin turned a bit more ruddy under the shadow of the day's growth of beard. "That was another lifetime." He looked to his wife then, and the expression on his face held so much love, a physical pain tightened Tori's chest.

Other than the pair of newlyweds they'd met in travels to this place, she'd never seen a man show that depth of care, that much undiluted love for his wife. And what the young couple in Pennsylvania had displayed didn't hold the maturity between these two. As if they knew each other's deepest secrets and loved even more for it.

She looked down at her plate.

"Bread?" Ezra's voice warmed her ear, and she nodded.

She took the tray, pulled one slice of bread off, and passed the tray to Opal.

"Jam?"

Again she took the offering, this time returning what she hoped would pass for a smile. "Thank you."

Serving by serving, she filled her plate, and it wasn't until she scooped the beans that she realized Ezra was feeding the dishes to her before he filled his own plate. She held her tongue, though, as her dish was now full and his was well on its way to being the same.

Taking up her fork, she sampled her first bite of pheasant, then breathed a sigh as the flavors melded on her tongue. Better than anything she'd experienced since leaving Pennsylvania. The simple beans accented the perfectly browned meat. And her next bite was even better, with the sourdough bread's crusty exterior and spongy inside blending with the blackberry jam.

"Your cooking is excellent, Mrs. English." She glanced at the woman, who didn't seem to feel the same about her meal, as she'd barely touched the scant amount on her plate.

"Please call me Mara, and thank you." She offered a tired smile. Her skin had lost any color she'd gained before.

Maybe it was the suspicious nature she'd honed since her parents deserted her just before her tenth birthday, but Tori couldn't help the needling thought that things weren't quite as perfect as they seemed with Mara English.

CHAPTER 5

"Would you ladies like to get some air? The moon's bright enough I can show you around the place." Ezra glanced between the cousins as they looked to each other. They seemed to be almost unable to act without the other's consent. Maybe that was an effect of whatever they'd been through, but hopefully he could get them talking as they strolled to the riverside. The Sweetwater sometimes had a magical effect, lulling a body into the feeling that all was right with the world.

Miss Opal Boyd was the first to speak. "I should stay and help Mrs. English clear the table." She kept her voice low, although Mara had stepped outside so his sister wasn't in danger of overhearing.

A niggle of reality tugged at him, and he glanced at the clutter of used plates and food leftovers filling the table. "I suppose we can wait until after. I'll pitch in, too."

He started to roll his left sleeve but paused as Opal spoke again.

"Tori can go with you. There's not enough room here for all of us to work in the kitchen. We'd just be tripping over each other."

He turned back in time to see another look pass between the women, this one bearing more than a simple question. He couldn't quite decipher the message, though.

Tori turned to him and seemed to square her shoulders for a challenge. That was something he'd seen her do several times throughout the afternoon. Traveling so far on their own, and especially into this untamed land, must surely require gumption. But the arch of her spine seemed to say more than that. As if she expected the worst to strike at any moment, and she planned to meet the blow head-on. Did she always plan for a battle?

"I'd like to see around the place."

Even her declaration held a hint of challenge, and he was caught between a grin at the amount of pluck she possessed and the urge to sigh and shake his head. What exactly had he gotten himself into with this pair?

He opened the door and allowed Tori to pass in front of him, pulling his coat tight around him against the icy air on the porch. "I can show you the barn and outbuildings if you'd like, but the moon's bright tonight, so the river's worth seeing first." His breath formed a dense cloud in front of him.

Her focus turned toward the distant water, but the shadows from the porch roof concealed her expression. Her chin bobbed in what might have been a nod, and she stepped toward the stairs. "Is the water very cold yet?"

He followed her lead. "Not as icy as it'll be after this snow hits."

"When do you think the snow will start? Will there be much?"

"Anytime tonight. And, yes, this looks to be just short of a blizzard." His gaze tracked northwest, the trees around the clearing blocking all but the tips of the distant mountains. "My brother Zeche is up in the mountains. I hope he's found someplace to wait out the storm."

"I wondered where he was. From your letters, I thought you both manned the stage stop together."

"We do. But he's taken the winter to explore the mountain country." And he couldn't help the tension in his chest as an image of Zeche's frozen body flitted through his mind. But that was silly fear. If any man was capable of surviving, nay thriving, in the wilderness, it was Zeche. He'd always had an uncanny talent for reading nature and falling into harmony with its cadence.

"Do you think he'll be all right?" Tori's voice had softened beside him as their steps slowed to a stroll.

"I can only pray he will."

She was silent then, and he didn't know her well enough to imagine what she might be thinking. Perhaps this was a good segue to ask about her home and life. "In one of your letters, you mentioned you'd recently taken over your family home, once you came of age. Have you found someone to care for the place while you're away?"

"I believe so. There was a family that lived there until my eighteenth birthday. I imagine they'll take up residence again."

He tried to weigh her words—her tone—for any tinge of bitterness. What had made them run? Would he scare her away if he asked outright? Maybe. And he couldn't risk them leaving. Not with the assortment of ruffians and derelicts scattered among the good people in the surrounding areas. There was too much chance they'd be taken advantage of by the wrong man. And that thought weighted his gut like a rock-hard biscuit, left in the oven twice too long.

"You said you might like to open a bakery. Have you done that sort of thing before?" They'd reached the river now, and slowed to a stop. The moonlight glittered over Tori's forehead and cheeks, deepening the shadows of her eyes. Illuminating the mystery that was this woman with the fiery curls.

"Not as a business, but Opal and I worked with her father's French chef many afternoons. I think we could turn out acceptable fare." A bit of defensiveness slipped into her tone.

"I've no doubt." He rushed into the words, trying to set her at ease again. "I'm just not sure we have enough people in the area to provide the patrons you would need. Is there another line of work you might consider?"

A sound emanated from her that he might have called a snort, were she less refined. She turned to look at him, but the action deepened the shadows over her face so he couldn't find her expression. Almost as if she had none. "We aren't selective, I can assure you. Any respectable line of work where we'll be safe and within easy distance of each other will suffice. We've both been well-educated, first in the Boiling Springs School for Girls and then by private tutor. We're qualified for hire as governess, cook, seamstress, or maid of all work." The moonlight glinted off her jaw as it flexed. "If you have recommendations about which towns might be our best course, I would appreciate the information."

A definite sting to her words, and it was high time he reined in her expectations. He schooled his tone into a light drawl. "Tori. I plan to help, don't worry on that score."

She made a sound, as if drawing in a breath. Was she about to cry? Surely not this strong woman. But she had been through an awful lot lately. His chest tightened. *Lord, don't let her cry.* He'd never been good with weeping women.

He pressed on, hoping he could carry her focus along with him and stem any emotion. "I'll ride to Atlantic City and South Pass to ask around. Those are the biggest towns nearby, so best to start there. If I don't find anything suitable, we'll just widen our search."

He watched her for a reaction, but she stood so still, she could have been a statue. At last, her words drifted through the night air, small and quiet. "You don't have to go for us, Ezra. I can do it."

Stubborn to the end. Yet he could hear the hint of uncertainty she tried to smother. "It's no trouble. I'd like to help. This is the least I can do for a friend." Those last words tumbled out before he thought through them, but as they resonated through his jumbled emotions, something about them rang true.

Whether or not she felt the same, he'd like to be Tori Boyd's friend.

"Thank you." She pulled her cloak tighter around her shoulders, reminding him of the cold.

"I should get you inside. The chill is deepening." He reached out and tapped her arm, an automatic gesture.

But she jerked back as though he'd burned her. Or slapped her. Had she been treated so roughly before?

She'd already turned and started walking toward the house, and her erect posture gave him pause again, as though she were running from something.

He forced himself to follow in her wake, his long stride gaining on hers. In the darkness, he couldn't tell for sure whether she was angry or upset or simply eager to get out of the cold.

A tiny motion of white in the air grabbed his attention. "I see our first snowflake."

That made her slow and look up as more delicate flakes salted the air. "Oh." Her voice held a bit of wonder, and she stopped completely to watch as the snow drifted down. Then, she tilted her face up so the moonlight illuminated every contour and she stuck out her tongue.

He stilled, every part of him halting except the hammer of his pulse. It took a long moment before his mind realized what she was doing. *Capturing snowflakes.*

Then she dropped her chin and turned to him with a grin that flashed a glimmer of white teeth. "Opal and I used to do that when we were girls." And then her smile faded. "Speaking of Opal, I should get inside and help."

He felt the loss as she turned from him and made her way up the steps into the cabin.

Yet as he stood in the cold, icy dampness pricking his face, he forced his mind toward the action he needed to take. If he was going to Atlantic City tomorrow, he'd need to secure help to man the stage stop.

With quick steps, he strode toward the porch, took the stairs, and crossed to the door in quick movements. He stuck his head inside. "Mara, would you mind coming out to the barn for a minute?" Josiah had gone there right after the meal, so that would be a good private spot for them to conference.

His sister looked up from where she stood by the stove scraping food from one cast iron pot into another. Her glance slid to Katie at the sink next to Miss Opal. The two looked to be washing dishes. Katie giggled at something Opal said, as the little urchin dried a plate and added it to a stack of clean platters. He notice Tori didn't spare him a glance as she wiped a cloth over the table.

Without a word, Mara moved both pots to the side of the stove where the heat would be less, then turned to follow him as she wiped her hands on her apron.

He held the door while she grabbed her coat and slipped outside. "It's snowing." He grabbed one shoulder of the garment to help her fit her arm in the sleeve.

"Katherine will be excited." Mara's voice sounded weary, softer even than her usual quiet tone.

He studied her as he followed her down the stairs, falling into step beside her on their way to the barn. "I hope Tori and Opal being here doesn't add more work for you, Mar. I was hoping they could help some around the place."

She glanced at him, but he couldn't see her expression in the shadows as they neared the barn. "They're already lightening my load. I imagine they'll have the kitchen clean when I go back in."

Good.

Light flooded them as he opened the big wooden door of the barn, and the inside seemed a haven without the wind that swept outside. Josiah's voice drifted from a stall partway down the aisle.

Ezra stopped outside the enclosure, propping his elbow on the door as Mara stilled beside him. Josiah glanced at them both, his gaze stalling on his wife before he continued brushing the chestnut he'd been riding earlier.

Then he turned back to Ezra, raising tired brows. "What's the plan?"

That directness was one of the things he could appreciate about his brother-in-law. "I need to ride west to find a safe place for the Miss Boyds. But..." He glanced at his sister. "I can't leave the stage stop and telegraph unattended. I imagine I'll be gone about two days."

She took his cue with a matter-of-fact nod. "Katherine and I will go over each day and take care of things while you're gone."

That was the arrangement they'd all agreed to before Zeche left for the mountains—if Ezra had to ride for supplies, Mara would fill in for him at the stage stop. She was competent with the telegraph—much more than Josiah—and had helped with the stages before she married and moved into her own home. They could leave the telegraph unmanned for a couple hours at a time, but not for the two days he'd likely be gone.

Yet still, asking for help nipped at his insides. He wouldn't do it for himself. Wouldn't ask at all if this weren't important. But Tori needed his help, and he couldn't deny a friend in need. Especially not Tori. Their letters had created a stronger bond than he'd realized when he'd been writing his and reading hers.

"When are you leaving?" Josiah gave the animal a final pat on the neck.

"I guess it should be soon. What works for you both?" Ezra stepped back to allow the other man room to exit the pen.

After latching the door, Josiah turned to lean against it. His gaze swept to his wife. "Is tomorrow all right?"

She shrugged, then nodded. "Should be fine. I did my baking here today, so we'll ride over to your place in the morning. Do you think we should spend the night there?" She directed her question to Ezra, but Josiah's presence seemed to grow as he edged closer to his wife.

Ezra spoke with confidence to soothe his brother-in-law's protective senses. "No need, just so long as you're there during the day for the telegraph and stage."

Still, Josiah slipped an arm around his wife's waist, giving Ezra a nod. "If we need to, I'll stay with them. We'll take care of things. Don't worry."

Mara shuffled her feet, then slipped away from her husband's arm. "I...need to get inside." Her face had gone pale, her eyes wide as if something urgent had overwhelmed her usual calm.

Before either of them could respond, she darted toward the barn door and slipped outside.

He watched her go, then turned back to Josiah. "Is she feeling all right?"

The other man was still staring into the darkness where his wife had disappeared. "As far as I know."

Ezra straightened and clapped his brother-in-law on the shoulder.

"Go on and check her. Get everyone settled in. I'll finish haying and head out."

Josiah seemed to gather his thoughts from wherever they'd scattered and turned to him. "Godspeed tomorrow. May He guide your search."

"Thanks." But as Ezra forked hay into the last of the stalls, he couldn't help the uneasy feeling tightening his chest. It was hard to believe any situation he found would be safe enough for Tori and Opal. The weight of their well-being was all on his shoulders now.

He'd wanted to have his own responsibilities, and they had showed up on his doorstep. But if he chose wrong in this mission, the results could be deadly for these women who trusted him.

CHAPTER 6

"I hate to drag you both out in this snow. You could have stayed back at the house."

Tori ignored Mara's comment as she craned her neck to see through the barren tree branches for a glimpse of the stage stop in the clearing ahead. The movement allowed a draft of snowy air to sneak between the layers of the scarf Mara had loaned her, and she curled back into the cocoon of warmth she'd created.

Between her and Mara, Opal hunkered down on the wagon bench, snuggled into Tori's side. "Coming to help is the least we can do. I'm sure you'll have your hands full with the animals and the stages with this weather." Opal had to almost shout to be heard above a fresh gust of wind whipping flakes into a swirl around them. Behind them in the wagon bed, Katie hadn't made a sound. Probably because she was curled under so many blankets and animal skins no noises would make it through the layers.

The horses plodded into the open country, and the buildings of the Rocky Ridge Station squatted low in the distance, seeming to be almost buried under the weight of the snow that had assaulted them all through the night. A thin trickle of smoke siphoned out of the chimney, attesting that it's owner had only recently abandoned the place. At least, she assumed he was gone. He'd told his sister he'd ride out at first light.

"Ho." Mara reined the team to a halt in front of the cabin. "You gals head in and stoke the fires. I'll put the team away and join you."

"Katherine can help me inside." Opal stood without waiting for a response. "Tori will go with you to the barn." Opal climbed over Tori so she could lower herself down the side of the wagon. She rarely chose to override a direct command, even one spoken as nicely as Mara's had been, but she made good sense now. Especially if Mara was in the family way, as they both suspected.

Maybe this land of tough people and even tougher wills was already starting to work its magic on her cousin. Although Tori hoped this place wouldn't change Opal too much. Her sweet-tempered innocence was one of the traits Tori loved most in her cousin, and it was a wonder Opal had been able to maintain such serenity of spirit while growing up in the den of iniquity she had. To safeguard that innocence was exactly why they'd fled.

After Opal had unloaded Katie and the supplies they'd brought, Mara drove on to the barn, pausing just long enough for Tori to jump down and fling open the large doors so the animals could stride inside.

Tori had occasionally helped in the barn at her uncle's house, so she was familiar enough with the harness to handle her share of the work. Ezra had been thoughtful to prepare clean stalls stocked with hay and water, although they had to break a layer of ice at the top of the buckets. Soon, she and Mara had the horses settled, and Tori held open the door for them to slip back out into the blowing snow.

Was Ezra traveling in this mess? She should have insisted he wait until the blizzard passed, at least. But that would have required her to know he was leaving last night, or even early this morning.

Which he hadn't told her.

She'd not known a thing until Mara began bundling her daughter this morning for the two of them to go. As soon as they'd realized what was going on, she and Opal had insisted on accompanying them.

43

Taking care of Ezra's responsibilities here was the least they could do while he was out seeking work for them.

She'd not meant for him to carry the weight of the search on his own. But since he'd taken on the load, she would let herself feel the relief of the lighter weight of responsibility on her shoulders.

Just this once.

When they stepped inside the cabin, warmth seeped around Tori, making her frozen fingers tingle inside her gloves. The sense of Ezra lingered in the room, and she looked around, half-expecting him to step out of one of the doors lining the back wall. Maybe it was his scent that laced through the place, comforting, invigorating.

Mara had already stripped out of her snow-dampened coat and wrappings, so Tori followed suit.

A clacking sound burst from the front corner to her left, and she turned as Mara strode toward the telegraph machine. She took up a pencil and scribbled furiously on a sheet of paper lying on the desk, and Tori couldn't help but step closer to study the noisy instrument.

If she focused, it was easier now to hear the difference in sounds that must be the dashes and dots. She closed her eyes and whispered each symbol as it came, counting on her fingers the numbers of dashes and dots before a gap of time must signal the end of a word. Or maybe that was only a letter. She had no idea how many of each made up the letters.

Opening her eyes, she searched the area for a chart that might show the special alphabet, but none revealed itself. Of course, Ezra had been so adept at his messaging, he clearly had the code memorized. And Mara seemed well-versed in it, too, as she settled into the chair and started tapping out a rhythm. Her fingers were a little slower and maybe more awkward than Ezra's had been, but it was obvious she knew what she was doing.

At last, Mara raised her head and looked around as she released a long breath. "There. We've received our token message for the morning. Traffic is usually slow through the wires until midday. What shall we do first?" She looked around Tori to where Opal and little Katie looked to be filling a wash tub with water.

"We're going to give the kitchen a good scrubbing. Katherine promised to show me where everything goes." Opal's face wore the no-nonsense expression that meant she was on a mission.

Maybe this was the time to voice her request, even though she should be taking up the broom to do her part in the rest of the house. "Mara." She took a tentative step closer to the machine.

"Yes?"

"Could you teach me how to use the telegraph?"

Mara's pretty brows rose, accentuating her wide brown eyes. "You need to send a message?"

"No. I mean…not really. It's fascinating." Her gaze traveled to the shiny metal of its parts. "I'd love to be able to work it. I find it amazing your mind can comprehend the tiny differences in the sounds, then translate them to letters and words while everything's coming so rapidly. I want to do that." She couldn't help the excitement in her tone. Mara probably thought her half-witted.

Ezra's sister was, indeed, looking at her with an indulgent smile, like a mother would give a child who'd declared he wanted to become president. "I see why Ezra's taken with you."

Tori stepped back. "Taken? No, he's just a"—she caught herself before she said correspondence partner and substituted a more general word—"friend." He was a friend. At least it felt that way after she'd read and reread his letters so many times, she'd memorized them.

Mara seemed to study her, and Tori turned back to the apparatus so she didn't have to meet the scrutiny in that gaze. "I know we have work to do first, but maybe if things quiet down, you can teach me the code for each letter?"

"Why don't we do a lesson now?"

Tori's gaze swung back to her. "Are you sure? Don't we need to start preparing for the stage?"

Mara shrugged. "I'll show you some things, then we'll work a while." She swung her legs under the desk as she took a fresh sheet of paper from a drawer. "The alphabet used for telegraphs is called Morse Code, and it looks like this."

$\sim$

 $\mathcal{B}$ y the end of the day, Tori would have expected weariness to grab firm hold of her muscles and weigh her down. Especially since they'd scoured the house throughout, using soapy water, rags, and the well-worn broom to rid the place of all the staleness of early winter. The snow had finally paused while she and Mara finished settling the horses from the last stage, and a murky dusk palled the air through the open barn door.

"I guess we'd better get our team hitched. Josiah will come looking for us if we're not home by dark." Mara's voice held an exhaustion that seemed to drain the strength from her shoulders, confirmed by the yawn that she covered with a gloved hand. "Excuse me. I'm not sure why I'm so tired today."

"Probably because you've been working so hard." Tori fought the grin tugging at the corners of her mouth. "Someone in your condition needs to rest more than you have."

Mara spun to face her. "My...what do you mean?" Even in the shadowy light of the barn, she could see the red surging to Mara's cheeks.

"We're right, aren't we?" Doubt niggled for the first time since she and Opal had discussed it the night before. "You're in the family way?"

Mara's lip slipped between her teeth. "Is it that obvious?"

Happiness bubbled in Tori's chest for her new friend. "You seem to get sick so quickly. When will the baby come?"

"Around June, I think." She dipped her chin and toed the packed, frozen dirt on the barn floor. "I haven't told Josiah yet." The words slipped out barely louder than a whisper.

"You haven't?" She didn't mean to sound so incredulous, but the interactions she'd seen between the couple thus far were so tender. She'd not expected this reaction from Mara. Apparently, marital unrest could be covered up as well out here in the west as it could in Pennsylvania. She shouldn't be surprised.

Mara shook her head but didn't look up from her muddied hem.

"Do you think he'll be angry?" A sudden urge to protect Mara washed through her. The same sensation that filled her every time she thought of Opal's tears after Jackson accosted her. That and the rage that still had the power to heat her veins in a second.

But Mara's sharp intake of breath caught her attention, stilling her throbbing pulse as she studied Mara's liquid gaze. "Angry? No, Josiah will be thrilled. I just…I wanted to tell him in a special way. And I've been so unsettled, I don't want him to worry."

Tori struggled to steady her pulse and focus on what Mara was saying. "You think he'll be happy?"

A smile bloomed over Mara's face, making her look no older than Tori, even though the woman must be ten years her senior. "Elated. But if I know Josiah, he'll be a little overprotective. Especially if he senses something is wrong."

Tori scanned her face. "Do you think something is wrong?"

Mara's teeth nibbled her lower lip again. "I don't know. I don't… think so, but…" Then she threw up her hands, heaving out a breath. "What do I know? My mum died when I was little, and I barely ever see a woman out here, much less a doctor."

She squared her shoulders, tightening her jaw in a determined look. "I'll tell Josiah tonight. It's not fair to keep it from him, and likely everything's going just as it should."

Tori pressed her lips together, an idea taking shape that had been pricking at her mind all afternoon. "Tonight then. And Opal and I will stay here so you have a nice quiet evening together."

Mara's jaw dropped, her brows forming twin lines. "What? No. Tori, I didn't mean that. I'll have plenty of time to tell Josiah. You're not in the way. We're *glad* you and Opal have come."

A rush of warmth flooded her chest at Mara's hurried assurances. She reached out to squeeze Mara's hand, a touch she never offered anyone except Opal. Yet, she had to still Mara's concerns. "It's all right. Please. I was actually thinking it would be better if we stayed here anyway. I'd like practice on the telegraph, and if any messages come through, maybe I can help with them. We can keep the fire going and feed the animals in the morning. You won't have to come over at all tomorrow if you'd rather not."

When Tori finally paused to check Mara's reaction, she was just watching her, a soft smile playing at the corners of her mouth. Silence settled over them for a second, and Tori finally broke it. "It's a good idea, isn't it?"

Even in the waning light, she could see the twinkle that touched Mara's eye. She grabbed both of Tori's hands. "I'm glad you've come, Tori Boyd. You're exactly what we needed around here."

The words caught her so off guard she could barely absorb them. She didn't even resist when Mara pulled her into a soft embrace.

"Thank you." Mara's breath ruffled her messy curls, and Tori slowly raised her arms to return the hug.

If she wasn't careful, she might just come to care for these people more than she meant to. More than was safe.

CHAPTER 7

*E*zra pushed Aristotle into a canter as the ground leveled out before them, and the road cut wide through a scrawny forest. The snow looked to be almost two feet deep in this open section, but at least no more had come down on this ride back from South Pass City. The ride out the previous morning had been miserable, and he'd made poor timing, not arriving at Atlantic City until close to noon.

It hadn't taken long to ask around, though, and the news was just as he'd expected. No decent work for honest women in these parts. Not unless they planned to marry up. He'd tried to phrase his question in a way that made it clear both ladies were moral and not looking to wed, but he'd still had no less than five marriage proposals. All five had offered to keep both women on as long as one would be willing to "tie the knot."

Over his frozen and lifeless body.

Because as long as he breathed, he'd not put Tori or Opal in a position that required them to either wed or go hungry. And he wasn't even sure he felt comfortable with the men offering to marry them. Marriage was a permanent arrangement, and he knew well enough that a person shouldn't go into it lightly or on a whim. Pa had instilled that wisdom in all of his children, refusing to even consider remarriage after Mum died, even though he'd lived a dozen years longer.

Mara had taken Pa's advice, and she and Josiah were so sappy over each other it was hard to watch sometimes. He might not want to be quite that smitten, but he'd like to at least have some feelings for the woman if he ever married. Be sure they were compatible.

Both Tori and Opal deserved the same opportunity.

The trees on either side of the road opened into the wide stretch of land around the stage stop as the buildings came into view about a hundred yards ahead. Smoke drifted lazily from the chimney of the house. Mara must still be there, although the dusky light of evening was falling quickly. Hopefully, she hadn't had trouble with the stages. With this snow, it was quite possible they'd been late, leading to a long day for her. Maybe she'd left Katie home with Josiah and the Miss Boyds. Or even better, maybe Josiah had come with her to help at the stage stop. With snow this deep, he wouldn't be able to work their horses in training, and he likely wouldn't have let Mara come alone while he stayed home in their snug house. He wasn't versed in operating the telegraph, or he could have handled all the responsibilities by himself, but the two of them would likely enjoy working the place together.

He rode up to the door, dismounted, and dropped his reins for the gelding to stand and wait for him. If Mara was alone, he would escort her back home before he tucked the horse in for the night.

The click of the telegraph wire sounded above him, pulling his gaze up to the corner of the roof where the wire fed into the house. Mara would be focused on receiving the message, so he'd do well to alert her of his presence carefully so he didn't startle her.

He let his boot sound on the snow-covered stoop, then tapped on the door before pulling it open. "It's just me." He kept his voice dimmed and glanced toward the telegraph as he stepped inside.

She was hunkered over the desk, scribbling on a sheet of paper, but something about the picture didn't seem quite right. The lantern sitting on the desk illuminated her face, shining through the cascade of hair that draped down to cover her cheek. The light gave the curls a reddish hue, and for a moment, his wayward heart lurched as his eyes saw Tori instead of Mara. But Tori wouldn't be taking down a telegram.

"Mr. Reid. Welcome back."

He turned to the voice, stilling at the sight of Opal working at the cook stove.

"I have coffee hot for you, and some stew just about ready. Come in and warm yourself and I'll set your place." She offered a comfortable smile, as though he'd stepped into her house, not his own.

He nodded. "Howdy, Miss Opal." And if she were here, maybe... He turned back to the telegraph, and finally believed what his eyes had been trying to tell him. That was Tori recording the message from the telegraph.

The clicking of the machine stopped, and she pressed her finger to the lever and sent the acknowledging reply, then straightened and looked up at him.

"Welcome home, Ezra." The smile lighting her face did little to still the rapid thump in his chest as he strode toward her.

"Where's Mara?"

Her smile dimmed, and the shadow that veiled her eyes made him realize how strong his tone had been. But where in west *was* his sister? Had she taken ill? Maybe the pallor of her face the other night had been a symptom of something awful.

He stilled in front of Tori and squatted beside the desk so he didn't tower over her. "Is my sister ill?"

The shadow shifted to confusion in her gaze, then wariness. "Not ill, no." But there was something in her eyes.

"Where is she? What's wrong?" His muscles tensed, ready for action. He wasn't a doctor, but he'd read all the medical books he could get his hands on, so the family usually looked to him when someone took sick.

"She's at home, I believe. Opal and I have been taking care of things here."

He drew back. "She left you here alone?" Something really was wrong with Mara for her to abandon her responsibilities like that, even though they weren't really her responsibilities anymore. She'd agreed to help, and she wouldn't fail him if it were in her control. She knew how important both the telegraph and the stages were to their livelihood.

He pushed to his feet and turned back toward the door. "I'll saddle your horses. Pack your things, and let's hit the trail."

"I need to send this message first." Tori's words halted him.

He turned back to her. "I'll do it."

She straightened, bristling like a frightened porcupine. "I can send it."

She could? He must have given her a dubious look, because she stiffened her back even more. "Mara taught me how to work the machine. I'm not as quick as you, but I can send the message. It's a short one."

His gaze dropped to the paper and he stepped closer to read the print. A pang hit his chest at the familiar script, the same hand he'd studied on each long-awaited letter. This time the writing wasn't quite as tight and uniform, obviously scrawled in a hurry, but it softened his guard a little.

He looked up from the paper to meet her gaze—and it was his undoing. The liquid amber of her eyes watched him with an intensity, a longing he was powerless to deny. "Are you sure you can?" The words came out a little too breathless, probably from the weight smothering the air in his chest.

"I've been practicing for two days straight." Her words came out a little breathless? The power of her gaze locked him in place, turning his mouth to a desert. She was so beautiful, more than he ever could have imagined. The fire in her hair perfectly matched the strength in her eyes, yet they seemed to frame the delicate touch of her features. The pert nose, soft lines of her chin, and her skin...so creamy his fingers tingled with the desire to reach out and stroke the length of her cheek.

A noise sounded behind him, sending his heart to his throat as he jerked away from her. His hand hovered mid-air. Had he actually reached for her? He stepped back. Turned toward the noise.

"Sorry about that." Opal gave them a sheepish look as she settled the tin lid on a roasting pan.

A sigh sounded behind him, and he knew exactly what Tori must feel, because the same action eased his own chest. He needed to back away, get some air.

"Go ahead and send that telegram." He swiveled and headed toward the door. Then he looked to Opal. "What do you need carried outside?"

The clicking of the telegraph sounded from the corner, and his mind followed the message as she tapped it. Slower than he or Mara would have done, but not very clumsy. The message was only a couple stilted sentences, but long enough that he missed the first half of Opal's response.

"…and should be here any minute." Opal turned to look at him as she finished.

He squinted to focus on Opal, scrambling to remember anything she'd just said. Nothing had penetrated, though.

"So we expect Mr. English with the wagon around dusk. I have our supplies packed." The corner of her mouth curved in a secret smile, and he had the unmistakable feeling she'd just repeated herself for his sake.

He ducked his chin as heat flamed up his neck. "All right." So if Josiah was coming to pick them up, he wouldn't need to hitch his own wagon. And now that Tori had successfully sent that message, he'd do well to get out of there before he made a bigger fool of himself.

He charged for the door. "I'll go see to my horse then."

The blast of icy air was almost enough to cool the heat of Tori's gaze as it followed him outside.

~

*D*espite what had happened between them by the telegraph machine—and she wasn't prepared to try to name it—Tori had to know what Ezra had found on his trip.

She paced the length of the cabin, fighting the urge to charge out to the barn and question him. But why was she fighting it? Ezra wouldn't be upset if she asked. After all, his news had everything to do with her and Opal.

Yet something about the way he'd stalked out of the cabin set her nerves on edge. She wrapped her arms around herself and went to look out the window.

"What are you worried about?"

She almost jumped at Opal's words, so close to her ear. She'd not even heard her cousin approach. Turning to offer as much of a smile as she could muster, she wrapped her arms tighter around her middle. "Not worried. Just wondering what Ezra discovered. I think I should go out to the barn and ask him."

Opal sent her an ambiguous smile. "He seems like a good man."

Tori turned back to the window to hide the warmth creeping into her face, although where it stemmed from she couldn't have said. "I think so." *I hope so.* They'd come an awfully long way because of that hope.

A man's voice sounded outside, and they both stepped closer to the window to peer around the yard.

A wagon. Mr. English sat on the bench, driving a team of matched chestnuts. The snow had started again, blowing sideways to blur the view of the rig.

"Looks like our ride is here." Opal turned to gather her coat and the supplies she'd stacked on the table.

After donning her own wraps, Tori reached for the door.

It pulled open before she could grip the handle, and she stood face to face with Ezra, just inches from his ruddy cheeks and wind-reddened nose.

She jumped back, and he stepped inside. "This everything that goes?" He motioned toward the crate, the only thing on the table.

"Yes, sir." Opal's quiet voice could barely be heard above the wind kicking up through the open door.

This was her chance. Tori pressed the door closed to block out the wind. "Ezra, you never told us about the success of your trip. Have you found positions for us?" She'd knew better than to think the churn in her stomach stemmed from excitement. His response could possibly seal Opal's future.

He turned with the crate in hand to face her. "Nope. No one looking for a woman to hire on." He said it so matter-of-factly, as if he were discussing what he wanted for dinner.

The sting of tears burned in her throat, but she stuffed them down, anger infusing her with strength. "Were there any jobs for men that we could train for? We're as able-bodied as anyone." But even as she spoke the words, her mind screamed that she would never allow Opal to perform a man's work. It would expose her to so much of the nastiness of a man's world. No matter how the male gender tried to present a cultured front in public, almost every man she'd ever known had possessed lousy character.

Ezra seemed the exception, but then, she didn't know him well enough.

When she met his gaze, it's brown depths had softened, and she swallowed down another knot in her throat.

"I wouldn't trust any of the men hiring, even though you likely could do most of the work." His voice had softened to an almost intimate level. "I'm afraid you might find yourselves in a situation worse than what you left."

She stiffened. How did he know what they'd escaped from? Was he just guessing or had Uncle Max somehow found them? If Opal's father had made contact with Ezra, would he turn them in?

She scrutinized him, yet his face remained open, earnest. No shift of his gaze that meant he was hiding something.

"Give me a day or two here to take care of some things, then I'll head north to ask around in Lawson and some of the other communities. That area's not as settled, but I still might find something. All right?" He reached out then, touched her elbow.

She almost winced at the contact, but she managed to hide it. She couldn't remember feeling a man's touch without pain of some kind, either physical or, worse, the deeper ache inside. Yet, Ezra carried none of the look that usually came with a touch. No glimmer of lust shone in his eyes. He might have meant it as a casual gesture, just a brush of his fingertips.

Yet no man's touch was ever casual. She'd learned that years ago.

"Tori?"

She shifted, and she wasn't sure if she'd pulled away from him or if he dropped the hand of his own accord. She caught a glimpse of the question in his eyes and looked away. Toward the door, anywhere but at the concern on his face.

"Is something wrong?"

She crossed her arms, building a barrier between them. "Nothing. Just let me know when you're ready to leave again. Opal and I will come back over and watch the place."

He let out an audible breath, but she didn't look to see the reaction on his face. "Let's say two days from tomorrow morning. I'll ask Mara if she or Josiah can come help you with the midday stage."

The last thing Mara needed was to come traipsing over here to handle feisty horses, but Tori could discuss that with her later.

The door gusted open, saving her from a need to respond.

"Y'all ready?" Snow cloaked Mr. English like an extra coat. "Storm's closing in, so I'd like to get home before dark."

She stepped after him out the door, but she glanced back at Ezra. His jaw held a firm set as he fell into step behind them, crate still tucked against his side. But when his gaze caught hers, she couldn't stop the flutter in her middle.

It was high time she got a handle on her emotions around this man. After all, any emotions directed at men besides anger and suspicion were dangerous.

CHAPTER 8

*E*zra soaked in the warmth of the sun for the first time in days, even though its strength lacked power against the chilly winter air.

This would be his second day home from the trip to South Pass City, and he had much to do if he planned to leave again the next morning. The house hadn't suffered at all in his absence—quite the opposite. The floors hadn't been so clean since Mara had insisted on a thorough scrubbing last spring. He'd spent much of yesterday in the barn, cleaning out water buckets, mucking stalls, replenishing hay stores from the loft, mending harness, and the like. Snowfall most of the day had kept him under shelter, but at least the weather was cooperating with him today.

He strode from the barn toward the house. Before he restocked the wood storage, he needed to stir the stew he'd left simmering on the stove. A glance at the sky told him the sun would reach the noon mark in another hour. The eastbound stage should have come by now, but the snow must have slowed its progress.

A movement in the distance snagged his attention. Riders. He squinted to focus on them as three figures separated from the tree line. The blues and browns of their clothing was barely distinguished against the dark background of the woods, and then a glimmer of auburn hair appeared. His pulse quickened. Tori?

The horses raised high hooves as they trotted through the snow, and he made out the figures of Tori, Opal, and Katie. He should have recognized his niece first from the showy patches of sorrel and white on her paint mare. But the draw of Tori's fiery hair pulled his gaze and held it.

As they neared the courtyard, he strode toward them, first meeting Katie's mare, Magpie.

"Uncle Ezra, we came to help." Even at ten years old, as the cares of hard work on the ranch were breaking through her childish innocence, her vivacious personality could pry a smile from him any day.

"I'm glad of that. What are we doing today?"

She swung down from Magpie as the other women reined to a stop. "Whatever you're doing. Miss Tori said you needed our help, so here we are."

His gaze swung to Tori, and she met it squarely, her lips curved in what could almost be called a smile. A determined one, for sure.

"We thought you might like extra hands, especially with the stages." She glanced around the mostly untrodden snow of the yard. "The morning coach hasn't come yet?"

"Not yet. Probably still wading through ice and snow." He reached to take the reins of Opal's horse. "Katie can help me get these ladies settled in. You'll find stew and coffee on the stove. It'd probably appreciate a stir if you get a chance."

The women slid from their mounts before he could step forward to assist them, so he did the next best thing and turned away to offer a little modesty.

The cabin door had barely closed behind Opal when another motion in the distance snagged Ezra's attention.

Finally, the stage.

He turned and strode toward the barn, pulling two of the horses behind him. "Katie, I've gotta hitch the teams for the stage. Can you unsaddle these gals for me?"

"Sure." She trotted to catch up with them, dragging Magpie with her.

His numb fingers fumbled with the harness straps, taking twice as long as normal to ready the horses in the icy air of the barn. He could hear the coach in the courtyard, voices echoing over the snow-covered ground. He needed to go take the incoming teams so the driver and passengers could eat and warm themselves.

He secured the last strap on Jack. "I'll be back in a minute, Katie." Then he jogged toward the outside.

The yard seemed astir with more energy than it had seen in weeks, and he sorted through the figures milling as his trot slowed to a striding walk. Tori's red hair was easy to spot in the midst of it all, speaking to a woman who leaned heavily on the arm of the man beside her. Tori reached out and touched the woman's shoulder, then motioned toward the house. The man and woman followed her direction as she stepped around them to speak to the next cluster of people.

"Reid. Glad you're here."

Ezra turned to meet the driver, who'd already begun to unfasten the horses from the rig. He stepped in to help. "Got a full load, I see."

"And held up at the twin buttes. Took all our valuables, but no lives lost."

He jerked up and stared at the grizzled old driver. "You were robbed?"

The man spat an angry stream. "Two ornery cusses all covered up with cotton sacks over their heads. Didn't have my guard 'aside me this time, so they got the draw on me."

Ezra's gaze darted toward the people trailing into the house. "Anyone hurt? How much did they take?"

"No one hurt, although the little lady swooned on us. If the word o' those miners can be believed, the snakes got away with close to a thousand dollars in gold dust."

His mind spun with the news. He should check the woman and make sure she wasn't injured. But first, he had to unhitch this restless team. "I'll finish here, you go in and get warm."

"It'll go quicker if we both pitch in." The man grabbed the lead horses' reins and led the pair forward.

Ezra glanced after the man as he worked to unfasten the rear horses. He couldn't even remember the fellow's name, had only seen him come through here a couple times.

They made quick work settling the horses, and Ezra clapped the man's shoulder. "Come in and fill your belly. I'll make sure everyone's comfortable before I hitch the fresh teams." Hopefully Tori and Opal hadn't been overwhelmed with so many hungry mouths to feed at once.

And then another thought stirred him. Hopefully the men inside weren't giving the Miss Boyds or Katie any trouble. There had been a stage full of people this time, and the driver mentioned at least two of them were from mine fields. In his experience, miners were often slim on manners. He started for the house, leaving the driver to trudge through the snow at his own pace.

When he opened the door, Katie's giggle met his ears. She had propped herself on the corner of the table next to the woman.

Ezra's gaze scanned the rest of the newcomers—six men in addition to the couple—and then landed on Tori and Opal, who were working in the kitchen area. Opal sliced something into the kettle, and Tori lifted the coffee pot from the stove and turned to the crowd. He would relieve the Boyds in a moment, but first he needed to check on the passengers.

"Any injuries that need tended?" He looked to the husband, flicking a glance toward the woman.

The man bent close to her ear and murmured something, to which she shook her head.

"None here."

The men seemed fine.

Thank God for miracles. He strode around the table to where Tori refilled coffee for a man in a buckskin coat who sported a thick, unkempt beard.

Ezra touched her elbow. "I'll take over."

She jerked her arm back and nearly splashed them both with the steaming coffee. "I've got it." Those brown eyes blazed.

He couldn't help but stare. Would she argue over a coffee pot? And why? He should shrug and turn away, leave her to the work if she wanted it so badly, but the reflex behind her reaction was so strange.

Before he could question her, the click of the telegraph sounded from the corner. It was barely audible over the murmurs and slurps of the people eating, but he'd honed his senses to pick up on the sound.

Tori looked like she would go to the device, coffee pot and all.

He almost touched her shoulder to stop her but stilled his hand just in time. "I'll take the telegraph, you serve the passengers." He turned away before she had time to argue.

It was longer than usual before the driver finally herded all eight passengers toward the waiting coach, which was standing ready behind the four fresh horses Ezra had hitched. But after a robbery and traveling all morning in the snow, he didn't blame the man for lingering over a hearty meal in a warm cabin.

The man and woman ambled behind the others, seeming to be deep in murmured conversation with Tori. What in the land of Goshen did she have to talk with them about? Did she have a prior acquaintance with these people? Surely that wasn't possible in a territory this big, but maybe they knew the same areas back in Pennsylvania.

He fell into step behind them as they passed the horses and neared the coach door. He wasn't trying to eavesdrop exactly, just going the same direction. But his attention pricked when he made out some of Tori's words.

"...take this to see you through to St. Louis. It should be enough to feed you until you arrive home." She took the woman's hand and thrust her closed fist into the palm.

"What? No." The lady stepped back. "We can't take your money."

"You just said the thieves took everything you had. You can't go without food in your condition. Think of the child." Her tone had taken on a tinge of frustration.

Ezra's gaze dropped to the fullish skirts hanging from the woman's high waistband. How did Tori know she was expecting?

The woman looked to her husband, uncertainty cloaking her face.

He seemed just as undecided. "We don't cotton to charity, ma'am—"

Tori extended her hand farther, cutting off the man's words. "Take this and stop arguing. Please."

A flash of mirth struck Ezra's chest, and he turned around so he didn't give away his nearness with a chuckle. Only Tori would be so blunt, even in her generosity.

"We're much obliged. Thank you." The man's reticence was clear, but at least he was willing to swallow his pride for the sake of his wife and unborn child.

When the sound of a scuffle signaled the pair were loading into the coach, Ezra turned back. Tori stepped away as the driver latched the door closed.

Then an idea occurred to him. "Hold on a minute longer, if you can. I'll throw some food in a basket for you all to eat on the trail." He spun on his heel.

"I already did." Tori's call stopped him mid-stride.

Turning back, he raised his brows at her. "All the extra biscuits and dry food?"

A flash of something passed through her eyes—worry? fear?—and then she raised her chin. "Yes. Everything in the pie safe and under that cloth on the counter."

All his baked goods for the last several days.

"Plus half the dried meat in the barrel under the work surface." Her tone was strong, almost defiant.

He nodded. "Good."

The driver climbed onto his bench, took up the reins, and offered a farewell salute.

Ezra returned a wave. "Godspeed."

And as the stage coach rolled away, his awareness shifted to the woman watching beside him. He couldn't believe she'd sent so much money with that young couple. Food for two all the way to St. Louis wasn't a paltry sum. From watching her mother-hen her cousin, he knew she had a kind soul under the layers she used to conceal it, but it took a heart two sizes larger than most to give money to a pair of strangers in need. Especially when her own situation was so tenuous. "Thanks for making sure they had food." He turned to look at her, ready when she flicked a glance at him.

That glimmer of concern—or something like it—swept through her gaze again, this time lingering in a moment of unguarded expression. "I hope I didn't overstep."

He took in the refinement of her features, perfectly blended across her face. "You did exactly what I'd have done, had I thought of it first."

Her eyes softened, and he caught a glimpse of relief. It seemed like more than just an easing of concern that he'd be angry with her actions. Almost like he'd passed some kind of test.

One thing was for certain, Tori Boyd was a woman of many layers, and he was finding her more intriguing with each facet he uncovered.

CHAPTER 9

*T*ori pulled her coat tighter around her as the early morning wind whipped her hood. Mara had insisted she borrow this animal skin wrap for the ride over to Ezra's, and now she was more than thankful.

"Think Ezra really left out in this weather?" Opal called above the sound of air blowing around her ears.

Tori scanned the river and beyond, as if she could see all the way to his cabin. But all that lay before them in the burgeoning dawn was white landscape. "He left when it was snowing last time, so I imagine so."

They reached the river, and she reined toward the spot they normally crossed when on horseback. The gelding Mr. English had saddled for her halted at the water's edge. She nudged him, and the animal shifted to the side, letting out a snuffle as he dropped his head to inspect the river.

She examined the water more closely herself, studying the way the snow seemed to blow across the surface in the dim glow of the sun that had barely begun to lighten the cloudy sky. Was the water frozen?

She slipped from the saddle and stepped to the bank's edge, then reached out with her toe to tap the surface. A solid top met her boot. "It's frozen."

Touching again, she put more pressure on the ice. A soft crack sounded and the firmness gave way slowly. "It's not thick, though."

"Do you think the horses can still cross?" Opal remained in the saddle but had reined her mare up beside the gelding.

"I think so." She grabbed a stick from the bank's edge, pulling hard to remove the end stuck in the ice. It pulled from the frozen mass, cracking another hole in the process. The sound of gently flowing water drifted up to her.

The branch was as thick as her wrist, and she used it to poke the edges of the hole she'd created in front of her. More ice broke off each time she knocked it. The stuff must not be more than an inch thick, and that was here at the bank.

She tossed the stick into the snow and turned to her horse. "I think we'll be all right to cross. We just need to work at it slowly. The ice breaks easily enough."

She mounted again, more than a little thankful for the trousers Mara had also insisted they borrow to wear in place of petticoats. She and Opal would have plenty of sewing to occupy them for the next couple of weeks as they stitched the clothing they'd not known they'd need here in the territory. But they wouldn't start that project until after they made it to town to buy material. Could furs be purchased to make a coat as warm as the one tucked around her?

"Come on, boy." She nudged the horse forward. Too bad she'd forgotten to ask his name.

The gelding took a tentative step, then lowered his head to snort at the water.

"It's all right. The ice will break as you step on it." Would the animal proceed, or would he be too skittish? The mare she'd always ridden at Riverdale would go anywhere Tori pointed her head, but it seemed this gelding required more convincing. Maybe she should pick up the stick again to break the ice in front of the horse as they crossed. It might be just long enough that she could lean over the animal's neck and reach the frozen water in front of its hooves.

"Do you want me to go first?" Opal offered.

Tori nudged the gelding again. "Let me try a little more. I think he just needs encouragement." As if he understood her words, the horse stepped into the water, splashing with both front hooves into the hole she'd created.

"Good, boy." She patted his neck, prodding him on with her heels. "Now lift high above the water."

Again the horse seemed to comprehend her exact command, raising his hoof so it just cleared the flowing river, crashing into the ice with the toe. The sound rang loud, even amidst the wind gusting around them. The horse jerked back, almost backing completely onto the bank.

"Good work. Good fella." She rubbed his neck, bent over his shoulders, crooning to calm him while she kept steady pressure on his sides.

With a combination of prodding and encouragement, they worked through step after step. Yet the going was arduously slow.

When they reached a third of the way across, Tori straightened from her position of encouragement. If there were a better way, she couldn't think of it. The ice was too thin for anyone to walk across, and there was no way to reach Ezra's place without crossing the river. They could always turn back and hope the weather warmed enough to thaw later that morning, but she'd promised Ezra they'd come at first light.

He'd not asked for that, but she'd offered just the same, and since she'd committed, he was counting on it. Especially after he said he'd be leaving out as soon as there was light enough to see the trail.

If he could do it, so could they.

"Do you want me to lead now?" Opal's voice was easier to hear since the wind had died down for a moment, and Tori turned back to her with a smile more reassuring than she felt.

"This boy's doing fine. I'm just giving him a breather." Her gaze dropped to the wooly bay her cousin rode. The horse stood in the icy water with its head lowered, as if dozing in the sunshine. The ol' girl looked to be as docile as they came, and Tori probably should let them lead. But she was the one who'd gotten them into this somewhat precarious position, and she hated to put Opal in the more dangerous spot.

She nudged the gelding again. "Let's keep moving, fella."

He balked, apparently not ready to end his respite.

She squeezed harder. "Giddup."

He rocked back on his haunches, then lunged forward, lifting both hooves out of the water in his rush. His hooves landed on the ice with a resounding *crack*, but the snow on the surface must have made the ice slippery, and he skidded forward.

Tori jerked the reins as the horse scrambled, trying to recover his balance. But the combination of the slippery surface and the splintering ice plunged the gelding down.

She felt herself falling, the horse dropping beneath her. A scream clawed from her throat as she clutched at the reins, the saddle, anything to stay upright.

An icy blast clamped around her legs, drawing her down into its lair. The horse toppled sideways, pulling her with him as the water soaked her hip, her arm, her side. She released the reins and clawed to stay upright, to keep her head above the water, even as it pressed all the air from her lungs.

~

The scream shot a chill through Ezra's core.

Mara, Tori, or Opal? He didn't stop to ponder, but images of each woman swam through his mind as he spurred his horse through the snow along the river's edge. The sound had definitely been made by a woman, and definitely from the direction of Mara's house.

He'd already crossed the river farther upstream where it was deep enough not to freeze easily, and had almost turned to the English ranch to tell Tori and Opal to wait until the sun warmed the morning before they rode to the stage stop. But he'd talked himself out of it because of the early hour. Surely they wouldn't be on their way to his place before daylight had set in completely.

As he rounded the curve of a boulder, his gaze captured the sight of a horse and rider standing in the river. In front of them, another horse seemed to writhe in the water. Where was its rider?

He urged his horse faster, intending to plow right into the river. But Dancer skidded to a stop at the bank, and Ezra clutched the horn to keep from catapulting over his head. The momentum helped him leap to the ground and plunge into the river.

His boots bogged heavy in the water, slowing him enough to realize it was Opal on the horse. She looked about to climb down.

"Stay in the saddle!" he yelled, slogging around her horse.

Something sharp jabbed his leg, then gave way as he pushed against it. Ice?

Tori was only a few feet ahead, splashing violently as she struggled to right herself. Her horse had clambered to its feet, blowing hard. Had it injured Tori during its exertions? Or were her heavy skirts dragging her down?

He slogged the final step, grabbed her arm, and pulled her upward. He almost didn't budge her, fighting a weight stronger than he'd expected.

"Ezra!" She grabbed hold of his arm with her other hand, pulling and writhing so much that she almost knocked him off his own feet.

"Don't struggle." He wrapped his free arm around her back, sucking in a breath at the icy chill of the water as he gripped her coat.

That seemed to be the leverage she needed to get her feet underneath her, and he was able to haul her upright. Between the fur coat she wore and the weight of her skirts, she almost lost her footing again. He pulled her to his chest, ignoring the frosty dampness that touched him anywhere his waterproof buckskin didn't shield.

She heaved in air, clinging to him. He pulled her closer, tucking his body around her. Savoring the feel of her in his arms more than he should. But the icy water still ran around their legs. "We'd best get out of the river." He spoke close to her ear so he didn't have to yell above the wind.

He couldn't tell if Tori answered him or if the sound she made was just the rapid chattering of her teeth. Motioning for Opal to rein her horse toward Mara's house, he kept his arm around Tori as he led her that direction.

She seemed unsteady, dragging all that weight behind her, and she'd started to shake violently. He had to get her into the house where she could change out of these wet things and warm by the fire.

He scooped her up, bracing his legs under the added weight. Water poured from her skirts, but he pushed on.

Tori clung to his neck, curling into him. Her nearness infused extra strength through his veins.

"I'll bring the horses," Opal called.

He only nodded as he charged up onto the bank.

∼

*T*ori couldn't stop the shivers wracking her body, even now that she'd changed into dry clothing and sat wrapped in two quilts beside the fire.

"I don't have tea made yet, but this coffee should warm you." Mara placed a saucer and cup in her lap.

Tori worked her hands from under the blankets, then wrapped them around the warmth of the tin cup.

The front door opened, and Mr. English walked in. Almost at the same time, Ezra stepped from one of the back bedrooms where Mara had taken him to change into dry pants.

She couldn't stop her gaze from following Ezra as he strode into the room, accepting a mug from his sister.

"Go sit by the fire and warm yourself." Mara motioned toward the chair opposite Tori. "Josiah, I'll bring you another cup so you can join them."

Both men obeyed Mara as though they were used to being bossed. Not that she was pushy, more like a mother hen.

Although Tori didn't miss the way Mr. English caught his wife's gaze and held it as he passed. The tenderness on his face was rich enough to make Tori's chest ache almost as much as it had when she'd felt the river closing over her. The obvious love between Mara and her husband seemed more than she'd ever thought possible.

Had Mara told her husband about the coming babe? She'd wanted to ask but had never found an opportunity when it wouldn't feel like prying. But something about his tenderness now made her think he must know. And he certainly didn't look angry about it. It seemed Mara had found the best of men.

If only there was another out there somewhere for Opal. Her gaze drifted to Ezra, settled in the arm chair across from her, staring toward the fire. He seemed cut from the same cloth as Mara's husband, perhaps an even finer model. At least based on everything she knew of him. Would he be a good fit for Opal? Perhaps she should broach the topic with her cousin, yet the idea of it started a churn in her stomach she couldn't completely contribute to almost freezing in the river.

Mr. English sank into the chair beside Ezra, giving her a welcome distraction from her roiling emotions. "Well, I'm awful sorry I didn't take you ladies to the stage stop myself. I thought about it but didn't figure it'd gotten cold enough for the river to freeze." He scrubbed a hand through his hair, then looked at Tori with sad eyes. "I hope you'll forgive me, Miss Boyd. I'll be sure to take you in the wagon next time."

"No need." Ezra spoke up before she could relieve Mr. English of his misplaced regret. "I'll not be heading out today. And I'll see them settled safely before I leave again, whenever that may be."

He didn't meet her gaze, but his words nudged her senses. Straightening in her chair, she eyed him. "Are you planning to go tomorrow then?"

He shrugged. "Maybe I should wait until the weather warms a bit. The cold and snow make taking care of the stage stop a lot harder."

"And when do you expect that to be, with winter just beginning?" She didn't mean her tone to hold such a bite, but honestly, they couldn't wait until spring to find work. That would require too much reliance on these good people. She attempted to soften her words. "If you'd rather not go, just give me directions."

The muscles at his jaw flexed, easily visible with the glow from the fire. "I'm not putting you in that kind of danger. You've been through enough already."

She let out a breath. "I made a mistake. I'm only sorry it put you and the horses at risk too. I've learned my lesson, though. I won't push the animals through an icy river again."

He looked at her then, and the depth of emotion in his gaze caught her breath. A combination of sadness and…what else? Fear? Longing? She didn't dare name it, but it captured her, nonetheless.

CHAPTER 10

*E*zra strode past the painted door of the shack that passed for a saloon in this hole-in-the-wall town. There couldn't be more than thirty people in the entire community, yet the ruckus inside made it sound like twice that number had piled in the place for homemade corn whiskey and who knew what else.

He left the building behind, heading on toward the room he'd taken in the boarding house. This was the second night he'd been gone, and the travel was wearing on him. Or maybe it was the way almost every man he spoke to about work for the ladies had some other kind of proposal to offer.

Some were respectful enough. Those who were married offered a brother or neighbor in need of a wife. The tavern owner he'd asked in the last town said he'd be willing to let the women stay above stairs if they'd earn their keep. The memory of it sent his blood to boiling all over again. He unclenched his fists, pressing the man's pock-marked face from his mind before he imagined himself plunging those fists into the crooked nose.

A ruckus behind him made him spin and reach for the pistol tucked in his waistband. Two men poured out of the saloon, rolling in a heap as one struck a fist into the other's gut. A third man ran out, jumping around them.

He started toward the group to help split the pair apart, but the blast of a gunshot rent the air. He ducked, running low to the corner of the shack. There'd been a flash of gunpowder near the third man, so it must have been he who'd fired the shot. Maybe even to break up the fight, but the whizz of air that had blown by Ezra's head meant the man was either a sorry aim or at least half drunk.

A burn singed his upper arm, and he felt the spot with his other hand. His fingers found a hole in his coat, and he winced as he touched bare flesh. No wonder he'd felt the zing of air from the bullet. A fresh flood of anger washed through him. He'd been on his way to stop the fight, and this was his thanks?

He peered around the corner of the building. A crowd had formed around the fighters, each man clamoring about what he saw. He probably couldn't pick out which of the men had fired the shot. The anger in his chest melted into disgust. He'd be leaving this place at first light, and good riddance.

Turning away from the cluster of drunks, he blew out a breath. Remote towns like this were the perfect place for criminals of all kinds to hide away. This was the last place he'd let Tori and Opal come, even if they were protected by menfolk he could trust. He'd let them wed one of the decent men he'd met yesterday before he brought them here.

Which begged the question, could marriage be the answer for them? He'd not broached the subject with Tori, but that seemed to be the only acceptable offer he could find. Maybe if he found the right fellows, it wouldn't be such a bad solution. Yet, he couldn't stop the churn in his gut as he thought of Tori with the gap-toothed farmer he'd spoken to outside of Lawson. Or the balding mercantile owner. Or the grizzly-like man who ran the sawmill south of that town. Any of those matches would keep her close enough that he could ride up and check on her every so often. And they'd all seemed like honest, hard-working men. So why couldn't he stomach the thought of it?

He should marry her himself and be done with it. Opal could stay in the spare room that used to be Mara's, and they'd both be safe.

He stilled, his hand on the latch string of the boarding house. *Could he marry her?* The thought hadn't really occurred to him, but...might it work? She knew him a whole lot better than she knew any of these other yokels, so she might consider it. Did he want that?

Letting the thought simmer, he pulled the rope and stepped into the dining room of the house. "It's Ezra Reid," he called into the darkness. "I'm just headed up to my room."

"G'night," the woman of the place called from the kitchen.

Trudging up the stairs, he made quick work of settling in for the night, then pulled the quilts up over him as he stared up at the dark ceiling.

Marry Tori. The thought sat better than any other he'd contemplated that night. And it would certainly solve her problems. Maybe she would see that and agree to the arrangement. If she wanted a chaste marriage, could he live with it? She was so beautiful, it would be hard to never touch her. But maybe, in time, she might change her mind. And as long as he could guarantee their safety—which he could do more effectively at the stage stop than any other place—he'd deal with everything else somehow.

Besides, if he had to take a wife, he could do a lot worse than Tori Boyd. She was as stubborn as her red hair portended, but in the couple of weeks he'd known her, he'd seen the depth of her caring, the strength of her devotion, the quickness of her wit, and the amazing speed with which she learned new things. The strength and animation of her personality would likely keep him amused for years to come.

No, it wasn't hard to imagine a life side by side with Tori Boyd.

~

*E*zra had pushed hard to make it back to the stage stop, but as he sat on his horse at the edge of the clearing and stared at the dark buildings in the distance, he was loathe to approach any nearer. Tori and Opal would have both gone to bed at this late hour. He should wait 'til morning to disturb them.

His breath formed a white cloud in the light from the quarter moon above. An owl hooted in the distance, and he strained to listen, waiting for the answering call. There hadn't been Indians in the area for a few months, but he'd learned long ago the simple sounds of nature weren't always simple.

He eyed the stage stop again. He should ride in so he was close enough to protect them, should danger of any form approach. The barn would work for him to bed down tonight, so he didn't disturb the ladies. Or the bunkhouse even. There he could light a fire in the little warming stove and shake off some of the chill.

Nudging his horse, they ambled forward, each step taking them closer home. He couldn't help the breathless anticipation in his chest as he thought for the thousandth time about how he would ask Tori. She loved letters, and the soul she exposed in her writing was what had first drawn him to her advertisement. Maybe he should write her a letter to suggest his idea.

He shook the thought away as soon as it settled. A man didn't propose marriage to a woman on paper, not if he could do it face to face. If he were to have any hope of talking her into the idea, he had to do this right.

He rode quietly into the courtyard and slipped into the barn. But when he lit a match and the lantern flamed to life, a chorus of nickers sounded from the row of stalls, erupting in the silent air. His own gelding responded, and Ezra stroked his shoulder as they made their way to an empty pen.

He had the animal settled quickly enough, made easier by the fresh hay one of the women had piled in the corner when they must have cleaned it. Just as he would have done. Had they noticed his habit? Or were they just that thoughtful?

Carrying the lantern that usually hung in the barn, he slipped out the door. Exhaustion weighted his bones as he trudged toward the bunkhouse, and his arm throbbed something fierce from the grazing of the bullet the day before. He'd ridden hard the entire trip, and a warm meal would be nice. But that wasn't to be tonight. At least he wouldn't be sleeping out in the snowy woods.

"Ezra?"

He stilled, then eased around to look toward the house. The voice had come so softly, he might have imagined it in his exhaustion.

But no. A beam of light haloed from the cabin's doorway, illuminating Tori. He walked toward her but couldn't remember consciously choosing to take a step. It was like she drew him. But why not? She was pretty enough to woo any man. "I didn't mean to wake you." He took the stair as she stepped back into the house, allowing him to enter.

"I heard the horses." She pulled a wrap tighter around her shoulders. "Come sit. You're frozen."

Maybe it was the yellow firelight inside, or maybe it was his senses dimmed from the cold, but a haze seemed to form around him, as if he were in a dream. He sat at the table where she motioned and took the mug she handed him. Strong tea spread through his senses, pulling him from his stupor as he breathed in the richness of it. The warmth from the cook stove finally began to penetrate his chill.

He straightened as Tori sank into the chair adjacent to his. "Where's your cousin?"

"Sleeping."

Of course. And from the look of her mussed braid, Tori might have been too. Although she wore a blue muslin dress, her face had a rosy sleep-ruffled look that built a lump in his throat. He fought the urge to reach out and touch her cheek. It would be soft, he had no doubt.

"Are you hungry?"

He was, but he was honestly too tired to worry over food. "I'll wait 'til morning."

"Was your trip successful?" Her eyes scanned his face.

Should he ask her now? Tell her his idea? No. He could feel the layers of trail grime covering him, and between his aching arm and

76

the exhaustion, he couldn't quite seem to clear his mind. Tomorrow he'd be better at finding the right words.

He sipped the tea again, letting its warmth soothe his aches. "I'll take another cup of this to the bunkhouse if you have it."

Twin lines formed between her brows. "You can't sleep out there."

He nodded, not up to an argument. "You ladies have the house. I'll be fine."

Her chin took on that stubborn jut. "You'll sleep in your own room. I'll move in with Opal."

So, it was she who occupied his bed while he was away. He'd wondered after that first time, when he'd inhaled the scent of flowers as he sank into the quilts. And the thought now warmed him with more power than the tea could ever possess.

She rose and moved to the stove, returning with the pot to refill his cup. "I'll slice some bread and meat for you."

"No." He reached for her arm to halt her, but the movement sent a shot of pain he wasn't expecting. He pulled back, fighting to hold in a grunt.

"You're hurt."

His pain must of have shown on his face, so he turned away from her probing look. "Only a graze. Not even worth talking about." His fingers wandered to his arm, covering the spot as if to protect it from her view.

"A graze? Like from a bullet?" The incredulous tone in her voice showed just how little she really knew about this wilderness.

"It's nothing." He swigged down the last of his tea in a long gulp, then pushed to his feet.

But Tori had already moved to the shelf where they kept the crate of medical supplies. "Sit down. Is the bullet still in your arm?"

He couldn't stop a chuckle, although it was partly spawned of annoyance. "It's just a graze, Tori. That means the ball never went in, only skimmed the surface. Just enough to get my favorite shirt bloody."

She spun, the crate in both her hands. "I'll deal with the shirt tomorrow. For now, sit down and let's have a look."

He couldn't have said why he obeyed. Probably the fact it was easier to concede than battle her, and he was so very weary.

"Take off your coat."

He did as she commanded, then loosed the buttons at his neck so he could slip the shoulder from his shirt. The wound was high enough on his arm she could see it that way and still allow him a scrap of modesty.

As the air reached the cut, its burn deepened.

Tori sucked in a loud breath. "Ezra, it's awful."

He glanced over his shoulder as she pawed through the crate. He'd not looked at the wound since the night before when he flushed it clean with water. He hadn't thought to bring a salve with him and surely wasn't going to bother the missus at the boarding house for something minor like this.

The gash had reddened considerably, and a thick white puss had formed around the edges. Infection was trying to settle in, which could be a danger if they didn't nip it at the quick now. "Let me have that garlic salve." He motioned toward one of the brown glass jars she'd set on the table.

She scooped up the container and stepped close to him, peering at his arm. "I need to clean it first, then we'll apply salve."

She started preparing the cleaning supplies, leaving him sitting there with his shoulder uncovered. For some reason, it felt like more of him was exposed than that bit of flesh, but he swallowed to still the uncertainty in his gut.

Returning with a basin of water and cloth, Tori knelt beside his chair and peered at the wound. She was so close, the warm brush of her breath sent tingles through his skin.

And then she touched the gash, clearing every happy thought from his mind. He clamped his jaw to keep from jerking backward. As she rubbed, he had to grip the seat of the chair to fight the pain. How could a little cut burn like she was holding fire to his arm?

"I'm almost done."

He tried to focus on her face, a welcome distraction from the pain she inflicted on his arm. Her brow had drawn together in a reflection of her deep focus, and she'd caught the corner of her lip in her teeth. He hadn't noticed before how perfectly shaped that mouth was—lips neither too big nor too small, but proportioned just right. Funny, he'd never given much stock to the shape of a person's mouth, but Tori had awakened him to many things.

"There." She looked up at him, her gaze meeting his in a way that stole his breath.

She was so close, just inches from him. Her wide brown eyes fathomless. So innocent, he yearned to touch her cheek, to draw her closer.

He reached out and brushed her soft skin. Was that a flinch? The movement was almost imperceptible, but he glanced at her eyes to see her thoughts.

A glimmer of fear shone there, stilling his desire with a strong fist.

He pulled his hand back. "Do I frighten you, Tori?" Bile had begun to churn in his stomach. Maybe he'd taken a misstep somewhere along the way.

A thin shield slipped over her gaze, yet he could still see through to the whirl of emotions she was trying to cover.

He hated to press, but he had to know. "Do I?"

"Not you." But the way she said the words seemed like she was trying to convince herself of their truth.

And then another thought hit him, a low blow to his gut. "Tori, has someone else frightened you? Another man?" He willed her to answer. To tell him what he was afraid to hear.

She dropped her gaze. Then seemed to catch sight of the cloth in her hand. "I'll salve the wound now, then wrap it."

As she turned away, a cold anger built inside him. "Tori. Who." He bit into each word, tasting its acrid flavor.

"It doesn't matter." She busied herself with the crate, examining bandages. But she'd revealed much with the flippant reply.

He softened his approach. If she'd been handled in a way that frightened her, the last thing she needed was him charging into the memories like a longhorn bull. "Tori." He kept his voice soft, relaxed.

She didn't look at him, though. Didn't even acknowledge his presence.

So he waited.

After a few tense moments, she turned with the medicine and a long white cloth. She focused on her work, not letting her gaze rise above his wound.

He let her work, careful not to concentrate too much attention on her. Not an easy thing with her so deliciously close. But the angry burn in his chest, the furious concern for her safety—her peace of mind—eclipsed all else.

At last she tied a knot in the bandage, and her quick movements bespoke the fact that she would likely turn and run the moment she finished.

"Tori." He couldn't stop the touch of pleading in his voice.

And maybe that was what made her stop. He would take her pause as encouragement to say the rest. "I don't know what's happened to you before. But you're safe here. As God is my witness, I won't let anything happen to you again. I promise."

She raised her eyes to him, revealing a wariness so thick it cloaked every other thought he'd hoped to read there.

He swallowed past the lump in his throat. What had been done to make her this skittish? "I promise, Tori." *Lord, help her believe me.*

She nodded, her gaze dropping to her hands. "Thank you." And with those words, it seemed like maybe he'd garnered a little of her trust. Maybe.

She rose, scooped the bottles from the table, and laid them in the crate. "I'll straighten this in the morning. You need your rest."

She disappeared into his room, leaving the door open wide. Within seconds, she reappeared with a satchel in her hand. She paused at the door to the extra bed chamber and looked back at him. "Good night, Ezra. Thanks for…everything."

He didn't try to stop her as she slipped open the door and disappeared inside. She'd come a long way in the last quarter hour. No need to push her further.

But as he sank back in the chair and scrubbed a hand over his face, he couldn't stop a sick feeling from settling in his middle. If Tori's past was as bad as he now suspected, would she accept his offer of marriage as a logical solution? He would have to make sure she knew he expected nothing in return.

Yet now, a deeper drive had taken root inside him. Not just to keep her safe, but to help her see that life could be...better.

CHAPTER 11

ori glanced at the closed door to Ezra's room as she stirred the porridge. Still sleeping? Or was he just hiding in there?

She couldn't clear from her mind the way he'd looked last night. The earnest expression pulling at his brows, reflecting in his eyes.

As God is my witness, I won't let anything happen to you again. I promise.

Those words had pierced her soul, reverberating through her veins in a way that scared her almost as much as those past terrors had. He seemed to be trying to say that she could trust him. Could lay down her guard with him.

But she'd sworn she'd never trust a man. Not any man. No matter how honorable Ezra seemed—and inside, she knew he was a man of his word—she couldn't let her guard down. The idea alone was enough to send her running.

"I'm going to feed the livestock." She whirled from her post at the stove and headed toward the door.

"All right." Opal's voice hung thick with question, and as Tori grabbed her coat from the peg, she glanced over to make sure her cousin had taken over with the porridge. Good.

She was gathering hay on the pitchfork for the last stall when the barn door creaked open. Tension fed through her shoulders as the sound of boots on the dirt floor told her it was Ezra. But she didn't halt her work. She would just have to pretend she didn't see him. That his very presence didn't quicken her pulse.

He stopped to pet the horse he usually rode, speaking in low tones as the animal greeted him over the stall door.

"I didn't mean for you to do my chores."

As she carried the fork full of hay to the end stall, she couldn't stop herself from glancing at him. His hair was mussed as though he'd just climbed from bed. A look more becoming on him than she would have imagined, probably because of the sculpted outline of his shoulders. His strength wasn't a thick brawn like a blacksmith or common laborer. He possessed a grace few men could claim, but Ezra's lithe movements didn't diminish his manliness in the least.

She fought a grin as she dumped the fodder in front of the eager bay. What would Ezra think if she told him her thoughts?

But that line of reflection would get her nothing but trouble.

He moved around the barn, and she watched from the corner of her eyes as he removed buckets from the stalls, dumped the soiled water, and carried them outside to refill at the pump. Watering was the last of the barn chores, so she could either help him or head back inside.

She couldn't say exactly why she chose the former, but working in tandem, they finished quickly.

"I smelled breakfast before I came out." Ezra latched the door behind the last stall and turned to her. "You hungry?"

She squared her shoulders as she preceded him out the barn door. "You didn't say if your trip was successful."

He was quiet for a moment as they walked, and for once she held her tongue. "I didn't find positions for either of you. But I did have an idea."

They were a dozen feet from the cabin now, and the door opened. Opal paused on her way out. "I was just coming to call you both. Breakfast will be dry as a desert if I keep it warm any longer."

The way Opal stood there, hand propped on her pert hip, forced a smile from Tori. Her cousin was coming alive in this place, finally resurrecting from the submissive waif she'd become under her father's increased domination.

After washing up, Ezra grabbed his bowl from the table and began to ladle gruel into it.

"I can do that." Opal reached for the spoon, but he held it away.

"No need. I'm as capable as you."

But Tori couldn't stop her gaze from sliding to his injured arm. Did it still pain him this morning? She'd seen him wince a time or two lifting the water buckets in the barn, but he hadn't slowed any.

They settled at the table, with Ezra occupying the seat on the end and Tori settled nearest him on the long side, Opal beside her. She folded her hands in her lap as she waited for Ezra to spoon his first bite of porridge.

But instead, he rested his arm on the table, hand outstretched toward her with the palm up. "Do you mind if I say a blessing?" He glanced at them both.

That's right. They'd been here so many days and she still hadn't become used to the custom. She glanced at Ezra's hand as she worked up the nerve to place hers atop it. It was a strong hand, calluses ingrained in the palm. Yet his fingers were long, probably what made him so quick with the telegraph key.

When she touched her palm to his, the warmth of his skin nearly made her pull back. And when he closed his fingers over hers, a tingle spread up her arm. Not a wholly uncomfortable feeling. In truth, not a sensation she'd ever experienced before. Certainly none of the times Jackson had touched her.

And the memory of the man took away all the pleasure in Ezra's touch. She forced herself to focus on his words as he prayed, barely remembering to bow her head.

"Thank You for these blessings You've given us, Father. For this food and the hands that prepared it. In Christ's name, Amen." His voice sounded so earnest as he prayed. As though he were face to face with his God.

They fell into silence as the sounds of breakfast took over. From the way he inhaled the food, Ezra must have been hungry. She should have fed him when he'd arrived the night before, even though he'd declined her offer. Of course he would have been hungry after traveling so far.

Which reminded her... She spooned a bit of gruel and looked up at him. "So, you said you had an idea while you were traveling? Someone else we could speak with?"

His head jerked up, his gaze darting from her to Opal. Did his face grow ruddy? That might have been a trick of the dim lighting in the room. "I, uh, I'll explain later."

He dropped his head again and scooped porridge into his mouth before she could respond. Poor man must be half-starved. It was better he eat first, then tell them when he could focus his thoughts.

When he'd finished his second bowl of food, he pushed his chair back from the table with a contented sigh. "That was the best breakfast I've had in a while. Much obliged." Then he rose. "I'll go hitch the team to take you back to Mara's. Shouldn't be longer than a minute."

"Ezra." She stepped forward to stop him before he left, but he didn't seem to have heard her. The door thudded shut behind him.

She turned back to Opal as she tossed her hands in the air. "I was going to ask him about his idea, but he seems in a hurry to have us gone."

Opal glanced at the door with narrowed eyes as she stacked the bowls and spoons at the table. "Go to the barn and ask him. I'll wash these and be waiting when you bring the wagon. Our things are packed."

She glanced at the table, already almost cleared, then at the work counter, free of everything that didn't belong. Opal had been her usual industrious self, leaving little for them to do now. She may as well talk to Ezra and make plans for them.

She pulled on her jacket and headed outside.

Ezra was leading two horses from the paddock beside the barn when she reached him.

She took the rope of one as he fastened the gate, then followed him into the barn. "What's his name?"

85

"Midnight." He gave her only a passing glance. "Katie named him."

The name fit the big black animal, although it wasn't especially creative. She patted the gelding's neck as they entered the barn, working up her courage for the coming conversation. When they reached the spot where teams were usually tied for harness, she was ready. "So, what was your idea?"

Ezra pulled the knot tight in his horse's rope, then looked at her. Something about his expression made the muscles in her neck and shoulders pull tight. Did he think she would dislike his plan so much? Maybe he thought she and Opal wouldn't be up for the challenge, whatever it was. Well, he'd soon find out they could handle most anything he threw at them.

"Tori, in all the towns I've been in, I've not found a place where I'd be comfortable leaving you. Somewhere I could trust you'd be protected and well cared-for. Not like I could give you here."

He paused just long enough for his words to seep through her mind. What was he saying? That they could stay on and work for him? Living with an unmarried man—unchaperoned? A knot formed in her throat, and she took a step back. She'd overestimated him. Trusted in his judgment more than she should have. No matter how good Ezra Reid seemed, he was still a man. Vile and lustful, just like all the rest.

"So I'm asking you to marry me, Tori. I could give you a good life, I think. Maybe not as fancy as what you had in Pennsylvania. But I would do my very best to keep you and Opal safe. And if you wanted to go back to your hometown, we could talk about it."

His words pummeled in such rapid fire she struggled to absorb each one, mostly because she'd stalled on the first sentence. *I'm asking you to marry me.* Even now, it's meaning wouldn't register completely.

His intense gaze pierced her, yet she couldn't bring herself to look away. "It could be a marriage in name only if you wanted, and I think I could make you happy. At least, I'd do my best."

Did he really want to wed her? A marriage in name only? What did that even mean? Of course, she knew what the words implied, but could any man remain chaste when wedlock removed all encumbrances?

She caught herself shrinking back, then straightened her spine to hold steady.

"It can be whatever you want it to be, Tori. I just want to give you and Opal a safe home." His voice had dropped to a low tone, gentle. Threatening all her barriers as her eyes began to sting.

She stepped back, shaking her head. "Ezra. I can't." She fought against the way her voice cracked on the last word.

"Tori, before you make a decision, let's talk about it. I think we can make this work."

She paused, breathing deeply to gather some semblance of control. He deserved more than three emotional words. Though he was a man, he'd given them shelter, never touching her in any way untoward. He'd traveled long, weary miles to find work for them.

And if his words could be believed, he was offering this union for their protection. He deserved a proper response.

Drawing herself up, she couldn't quite bring herself to meet his gaze. She locked her focus on his stubbly chin. "I appreciate your help, Ezra. Truly I do. But I won't marry you. I don't plan to ever marry, especially not now."

He was quiet for a long moment, and the burn of his gaze seared her face. She didn't turn away, didn't back down, just kept her attention fastened on his chin. The several days' growth shadowing the strong lines made her stomach clench.

If she were ever to let her guard down around a man, it would be this one.

At last, he blew out a long breath and turned away. "All right then. If you change your mind, the offer will stand."

And with the force of his gaze releasing her, she turned and fled the barn. Yet with every step, she could hear the disappointment in his tone. Had she made the wrong choice? Maybe she'd refused their best option.

She had to force herself not to turn and admit her mistake.

◦∼◦

*E*zra heaved out another long breath, frustration coursing through his veins. He should have known. She'd been exhibiting all the signs. She didn't want to be married to him, plain and simple. She'd said *I won't marry you*, but, really, she'd meant *I'd just as soon swallow poison as marry your sorry hide.*

And wasn't that always the case of it? His older brother Zeche had the fierce presence that demanded respect from the moment he walked into the room. Mara had spunk and caring that caused everyone who met her to become instantly enamored. And that left him, the baby brother, overshadowed and unseen.

This winter, he'd planned to make that different. To prove that he could shine in his own right, manning the stage stop and the telegraph without aide from the others. And the sudden appearance of Tori and Opal...well, they'd given him real purpose. They *needed* him.

Apparently, they didn't need him as much as he'd thought.

Woodenly, he finished harnessing the team and backed the pair into place at the wagon. He should send the women home to Mara's on their own. After all, Tori would surely have no qualms about driving the horses. She charged into every other task with reckless determination.

But he couldn't. It would be wrong to desert them just because his pride was wounded.

No, he'd make it through the trip to Mara's, then maybe he'd split some wood. Not that he needed the logs added to the full supply they'd prepared for the winter, but perhaps after he cut up a tree or two, he might be able to slice through the sting of Tori's refusal.

CHAPTER 12

"If you punch that dough any harder, you'll knock the yeast out of it."

Tori ignored her cousin's light tone as she gave the sourdough another sharp jab. "I'm almost done."

"And moody to top it off, from the sound of your tone."

She sent Opal a glare, but the look seemed to slide right off her cousin. "What has you so perky today?"

"You mean besides the fact that it's a beautiful day, the snow is melting, I just played a game of hide-n-seek with Katie, and not even your pining is going to steal my joy?"

"I'm not pining. What would I be pining for?" Although longing could be an apt description of the ache that had taken up residence in her chest.

It'd been three days since she refused Ezra's proposal. Three days since the long wagon ride where he'd sat in stoic silence beside her. Not once had he come by since then. He'd not come to check on them nor said when he'd head out on another trip to look for work for them.

Although, maybe he'd decided to stop the search. He did, after all, have a life of his own, with plenty of work to do—the stages and telegraph and all the animals around the place. She wouldn't blame him if he decided their battles weren't his to fight any longer.

Especially after she'd thrown all his kindnesses back in his face. But what choice did she have? She couldn't possibly marry, not even a man as good as Ezra Reid. And where would that leave Opal? Other than nicely settled in the extra bed chamber in the little house.

But what if Opal's father came to look for them? If they needed to run, she couldn't do so tied to a man. And it wasn't fair to uproot Ezra's life like that.

She'd already disturbed it enough.

She and Opal should just leave on their own, maybe rent horses from Mr. English and head west. Although perhaps that *would* be dangerous. They might do better to catch the westbound stage for a few days until they found better prospects.

"Penny for your thoughts?"

Opal's words pulled her from her mental wandering, and she forced her voice to relax. "I'm thinking it's time for us to move on. Maybe we should take the stage tomorrow and see if we can find work farther west. Maybe even go all the way to California."

She could feel Opal's gaze on her, and she looked up to meet her curious blue eyes.

"What makes you want to do that?"

What, indeed. She shrugged. "I just feel like we're an inconvenience here. I don't want to intrude on Ezra's good will any longer."

Her cousin was studying her with that intensity that could see through to Tori's every thought. She looked down at the bread dough she'd been fingering, rolling tiny balls between her fingers. She'd have it so mutilated soon, the dough would never rise.

"That feels a little like running, doesn't it?"

Tori sighed. "We're not running again. Not really. I just...there's not really a place for us here, and I don't want to cause any more trouble."

After another moment, Opal released a matching sigh. "All right. Are you going to tell Ezra?"

She swallowed. "Not until we're ready to board the stage."

"When will you tell Mara?" Opal always did have a knack for asking the tough questions in her quiet way.

"I suppose I'll tell her tonight. She'll probably be relieved, although she'll miss your help in the kitchen."

❧

"Opal and I are planning to leave on the westbound stage tomorrow." Tori studied Mara's reaction over the mending in her lap. The other woman's face lost all color. Just like it usually did before she scurried outside to lose her breakfast.

"You can't."

Tori rested the trousers with the gaping knee in her lap. "I think we need to. It'll be best."

But Mara was already shaking her head. "No, it won't. You two coming was the best thing that's happened to Ezra, and I'm not sure *I* can do without you either." She rested a hand on her flat midsection. "Besides, Ezra won't be back for a couple more days. You need to at least wait and see what he's found."

She eyed the woman. "Back from where?"

"He's gone south this time to look for work for you both."

Tori's senses sprang to alert. "Why didn't he say something? When did he leave?" Why hadn't he asked them to take care of things at the stage stop?

"He left this morning."

"What?" She laid the mending back in the basket. "Who's manning the telegraph? And the stages?" She glanced out the window but knew she wouldn't see anything in the darkness of late evening. "I'll pack my things and ride over there tonight."

"Relax, Tori. Josiah's been taking care of the place today. He took his training horses over there to work them, so he could be on hand for the stages. And he fed the animals before he came home tonight."

Her mind swam through all the other chores and responsibilities on the place. "But what about the telegraph? You said Josiah hasn't learned the code." And what if Indians attacked the place again? They could steal all the animals and burn down the buildings with no one to stop them.

And why hadn't Ezra come to tell her? It was only right that she and Opal take care of the station while he sought work on their behalf. In fact, doing her part was the only way she could rest easy letting him take on so much for her.

And why would he continue to help after she'd denied his proposal so adamantly? Not even Ezra could be so altruistic, could he? Did he think he would sway her into changing her answer? Men just didn't do this much to help another person—especially a woman, or two women—without expecting some kind of return for their efforts.

She studied Mara's face. "Why is he doing this?"

The other woman looked at her, head cocked as though trying to figure why Tori had to ask. "Because he wants to help." Her lips pressed together, and she dropped her gaze to the tiny baby gown she'd been hemming. "My little brother's always had a soft spot for anyone he can help. If he feels there's been an injustice done, he's the first to step in and make it right."

Was that what he thought had happened with them? He was right. And maybe that did explain his drive to help them get settled. But could any man really be that noble?

If it were possible for a man to possess that much chivalry, Ezra Reid just might.

～

*E*zra rode into the quiet town as dusk settled over the landscape. The neat rows of buildings lining the road were tucked like diverse packages, nestled in a line. One side of the street even sported a boardwalk part of the way. He'd not roamed this far west before, almost to the far edge of the base of the Rocky Mountains, so this hamlet had offered a pleasant surprise.

He reined his gelding to a stop in front of a blue, two-story building labeled as *Shumeister Boarding and Bakery*. Both notions sounded heavenly right now, since he'd slept under the stars the night before and had been eating dried tidbits from his saddle pack all day.

He swung down from his horse and bit back a groan as the action pulled at the muscles in his sore arm. That measly gunshot wound should have healed by now. At least, it shouldn't have still been shooting fire through his arm every time he used it. Of course, all his joints and muscles ached, which meant he was letting the long days in the saddle affect him more than he should. After tying his horse to the rail, he stepped onto the wooden walk and rapped his knuckles on the door.

From inside, a woman's voice sounded, along with the tapping of shoes on a wooden floor. He removed his hat and waited as the door swung open.

"Yes?" A lady peered up at him, short and stocky with a kind face and long gray hair pulled into a knot on the top of her head.

"Your sign says you might have a room to let for the night?"

"Ja. Come with me." Her voice was thick with some kind of accent. German? Norwegian? He should have expected it from the name Shumeister.

He followed the woman into a decent-sized dining room, where she bent over a desk in the corner, opening and closing drawers. "How long you stay?" Tantalizing smells emanated from an open doorway that must have been the kitchen, and his stomach tightened in a noisy grumble.

"Just tonight. Do you serve dinner, too?"

"Ja. In half an hour. And breakfast will be ready at first light." She slammed the last drawer and straightened. "I show your room."

She had an efficient, almost brusque manner, yet something about her face held a kind honesty. She led him up the stairs, but she'd not made it up half a dozen before she slowed to catch her breath.

He treaded slowly behind her. Her steady puffs grew louder with each step, and they'd only made it partway. "If you just want to tell me which room is mine, I'll find it. You don't have to show me."

A grunt was her only response, and she kept climbing the stairs. Ezra stayed close in case he'd need to catch the woman when she swooned from lack of breath. Her robust form must not allow for much circulation through her airways.

At last, they reached the upper level, and she led him to a neat room, better situated than any he'd stayed in since they'd moved out west. Blue calico curtains hung from the windows, matching one of the colors in the quilt spread across the bed. There was even a dresser that held a washbasin and pitcher.

"I fill water this morning." She motioned toward the pieces. "I call to eat when ready."

"Yes, ma'am. Thank you."

She turned and gave him a final perusal, scanning him from his mussed hair down his grubby clothes to the tips of his dusty boots. He did his best not to back down from her look, but he must appear like something the dog dragged in.

She gave a decisive nod, then turned and waddled down the stairs.

At dinner, he met Mr. Shumeister as well as the doctor who kept a permanent room in the place.

"What brings you to our little town, Reid?" The doctor was an older fellow with plenty of salt mixed in with his black hair and beard.

"I'm seeking work for friends." He shifted his gaze between the two men as he spoke. "Two ladies who've recently come west are looking for positions appropriate for their gender." He spoke the last words in a way his meaning couldn't be misconstrued. "They're happy to work as cooks or seamstresses or clerks. In fact, one of them is becoming quite adept as a telegraph operator."

The doctor's gaze took on a faraway look as he chewed his food. Mr. Shumeister took another bite of his ham and cabbage, not even glancing Ezra's way. He was a thin man with hair so blonde it was hard to tell how much was gray. His lined face kept a somber look, although that might be an effect from the mustache that drooped on either side of his mouth. The soft way he'd gazed at his wife as she brought a plate of sourdough bread from the kitchen had spoken well of the man's temperament. Any fellow who showed love for his wife usually possessed a good streak.

"You say the women cook. They bake, too, ja?" Mr. Shumeister's accent was almost as strong as his wife's.

Ezra nodded. "Yes." He hated to commit them to too much, but he'd tasted the pie Miss Opal made at Mara's one evening and could vouch for their baking skills.

The man glanced toward the kitchen, from whence occasional cooking sounds drifted. Then he looked back at Ezra and gave a curt nod. "We put them to work. Room and board, plus a dollar a week for each. They help my Aggie." Then he scooped a fork full of ham and stuffed it in his mouth.

Ezra sat back in his chair, eyeing the man. "You have enough work for them both?" With only one regular boarder, how could they afford to feed themselves, let alone two more women?

The blonde man glanced up at him, a twinkle touching his eye for the first time. "My wife, she bake for the town. Too much for only her."

Ezra let the idea develop in his mind through the rest of the meal. Could he picture Tori and Opal here? Maybe. The place was clean, the house well-built and obviously cared for. Mrs. Shumeister seemed like a hard worker and was certainly a good cook, as proven by the meal that both her husband and the doctor were presently scarfing down. And there was even a physician on the premises, in case either of them took sick.

He glanced at each of the men. Neither looked to be lecherous—more fatherly than anything.

He bit into his bread and forced himself to chew. This may be just the place he sought, yet how could he send the women so far away? Almost two days' ride from the Rocky Ridge. That would mean he might not see Tori again for months. Or years. Or never.

Yet, maybe that was best. She'd made it clear she held no romantic notions for him, made it clear she didn't plan to marry. Ever. So it was past time he squelch the affection that had grown too rapidly in his own chest. Ever since he'd had that blasted thought of marrying her, she'd taken over his thoughts more with every hour.

Maybe two days' ride would be just enough distance to purge her from his mind. And keep her out of his heart.

CHAPTER 13

*T*ori plunged the paddle into the steaming water, stirring the clothing, her mind churning as much as the wash. Her gaze wandered to the horizon, scanning as far as she could see in each direction.

When would Ezra return? Today made the fifth day he'd been gone. Mara hadn't said how long he planned to be away, but surely this was too long. Should they go look for him? She glanced toward the road the stage coaches took, then at the sky. The weather had been bright, if cold, for days now, so it couldn't be snow delaying him.

Had he been accosted on the trail? Or worse, what if he'd been killed? What if he'd been mixed up in another barroom brawl, and this time the bullet did more than graze his arm?

Her stomach swam with the images, with the thought of Ezra wounded and in pain, lying in the street or on the trail with no one there to tend him.

She scooped the gowns from the wash water and laid them in the clean bucket to cool. With a shove, she dumped the pail of suds over her heating fire, then scooped up the container of clean dresses and charged toward Ezra's cabin.

She was done waiting and stewing. If Ezra needed her, it was time to find him.

Opal stirred a pot of soup at the stove, the savory aromas drifting through the cabin.

Tori plopped the bucket of soggy clothing by the door to her room. "I'm gonna ride to Mara's. Something's wrong with Ezra, and I need to see where to start looking for him."

Her cousin dropped the wooden spoon onto the stove's surface. "Where is he? Did he send word?"

"No, but I can feel it. Something's wrong." Tori's mind spun as she stepped into the bedroom and grabbed her satchel, then the only other clean, dry dress she had here. What would she need to take on the trail? Food for sure, and blankets. Feed for the horse. Matches to start a fire.

She grabbed the handles of her bag, then snatched up two quilts from the trunk at the base of the bed.

"Tori, you're not planning to go look for him, are you?"

Opal stood in the doorway with hands on her hips, blocking her exit.

"Yes." She pushed past her cousin. "I'm going to Mara's first to find out exactly where he was planning to go. I'll see if Mara can come over here with you during the day to take telegraph messages. Then you ride back with her at night." She paused, then spun on her heel to face Opal. "Do not sleep here alone, do you hear?"

Opal's honey-colored brows raised. "So, you're going to sleep out on a trail where any savage or criminal can stumble across you, but I'm not allowed to stay in a perfectly safe cabin with a locking door?"

She bit back a growl then did her best to temper her tone. "Please, Opal. I can't worry about you, too. Sleep at Mara's. There's no need for you to stay here overnight."

Opal's tone softened, too, but only a little. "Don't worry about me, Tori, but I don't think you should ride off alone. Ezra's fine, I'm sure. I'll go with you to Mara's, and we'll talk through it together."

But the sound of hoofbeats caught them both up. Tori dropped her load and sprinted for the door. Ezra? Her heart leapt with the hope, yet she couldn't fight the dread balling in her middle.

Mara sat atop a flashy chestnut and white mare, Katie peering around from behind her.

Not Ezra. Her stomach plummeted as she stood on the top step. She fought to keep her back straight, the burn in her eyes at bay.

Katie slid down and ran toward them. "Miss Tori, we came to see how you're doing."

"Fine, Katie. I was just about to ride to your house." She swallowed, trying to wash down the lump clogging her throat. That instant of hope had come too close to unraveling her.

"My brother has still not returned?" Mara stepped forward, the horse ambling behind on a long rein. The compassion in her eyes and tone made Tori square her shoulders.

"No, and I'm going to ride out to look for him. I was coming to ask you exactly where he'd planned to go."

Alarm widened Mara's eyes, and she took a step closer, as though she would grab Tori's arm and keep her from leaving. Then she stopped and glanced around. "Katie, take Rose to the barn and untack her please."

After handing the horse off to her daughter, Mara mounted the step to the porch and did take Tori's arm, looping elbows in the way Tori and Opal had years ago when they were girls. "Let's have a cup of tea and see what's best to be done."

Opal seemed to be of the same mind as Mara, because she was pouring brown liquid through the strainer into three mugs as they entered.

Mara took a seat at the table and motioned for Tori to sit across from her. "Now. Have you heard from Ezra? Through the telegraph or stage?"

The thought of sitting down for a chat chaffed at Tori, but she reluctantly sank on the bench where Mara had pointed. "Not a thing."

She cocked her head, gaze distant as though deep in thought. "He said he was going to Rock Creek, then planned to stop in at some of the ranches west of there. He could have gone on to the mines near the mountains, and I've heard there's a town past the base of the range. Depending on what he found, it may take another day or so to travel all that distance."

Distress stirred in Tori's chest. "Something's wrong, Mara. I can feel it. Could you draw a map of those areas with landmarks I can follow?"

"I have a better idea." Mara pushed to her feet and strode over to the telegraph. She took the chair and sat, smoothing her skirts with a determination that emanated from her in waves.

Tori stood beside her, watching until she could get a grasp on what the other woman was thinking.

Mara positioned her fingers on the telegraph key and started a message.

Atlantic City, stop.

The acknowledging reply came almost immediately, and Mara pressed the keys again.

Searching for man named Ezra Reid, stop. Please inquire at hotels and boarding houses, stop. Please advise answer, stop.

Could that actually work? The operator on the other end acknowledged the request and promised a swift reply.

The next message she sent was directed to the South Pass City telegraph operator. As Mara received their agreement to assist in the search, Tori couldn't help the bud of hope forming in her chest.

She grasped her hands in front of her. "What other towns might he have stopped in?"

Mara sat back, her fingers drumming on the desk's surface. "Rock Creek doesn't have a telegraph, but neither do they have a hotel that I know of. There's a town farther west, past most of the mines." She leaned over the machine again, then started tapping furiously on the key as she sent a message to a place she referred to as Mountain Bluff.

Tori's pulse thrummed in her neck as they waited for a response. After several moments, Mara looked up at her, apprehension in her gaze. "I'll give them another moment, then try again. It's a small town, so the operator handles other jobs, too."

Like here. Tori's gaze wandered the room, taking in the details that felt so familiar now. So comfortable. More like home than her parents' house, where she'd taken up residence on her eighteenth birthday. And certainly more like home than Riverdale had ever been, even though she'd lived there almost half her life.

The telegraph sounded, jerking Tori's gaze back to it. The message was from Atlantic City, and Mara was furiously scribbled the text as it came through.

No man found by that name, and no unidentified persons at the hotel.

Tori swallowed down her disappointment as Mara repeated the message to the operator on the other end for confirmation.

Before she finished, though, another incoming message sounded. The telegrapher from Mountain Bluff was finally responding.

As Mara sent the search details, Tori turned away from the desk. Mara was the better telegraph operator, able to send and receive faster than she could, although she'd been working hard to increase her speed. But right now, she had other things to accomplish.

She headed to the kitchen, where Opal was wiping down the work counter. Her cousin gave her a questioning look as Tori grabbed several biscuits and some of the dried staples Ezra kept on hand. She wasn't sure exactly how far it would be between towns, but she should take enough food to last at least a day. She could replenish her supplies along the way, depending on where they located Ezra.

If they could find him through the network of telegraph lines, it would be a miracle. But she had to hold onto that hope for now.

"You're still going to look for him?" Opal's voice held a note of resignation as she reached for a cloth sack from a shelf.

"I have to. He would be back by now if there weren't a problem. And he's doing all this for us. I need to be there to help him." She pushed the food toward Opal, who began organizing it inside the bag. Then she reached for a canteen and poured water from the drinking bucket.

"I'll go with you then." Opal's voice held a strange matter-of-fact tone. "And when we find him, you may as well marry the man and be done with all this."

Tori sucked in a gasp, then choked on the air as it strangled something in her throat. "What?"

Opal didn't stop her work, didn't even glance at her. "You heard me. And I'm a little hurt that you haven't told me you're in love with him. Although maybe that's because you won't believe it yourself." Her cousin did turn to look at her then, her blue gaze drilling through Tori's defenses. "And Ezra's more than half fallen for you, Tori. That's plain for anyone to see when he looks at you. I know you're afraid to trust a man, but Ezra's different. Even you said so. I think you need to let your guard down."

Tori fought the urge to shake her head as the words escalated. Marry? No, no, no. Ezra *was* different. Honorable, even. But this wasn't about him. The reaction of her body and mind to Opal's words only reinforced the fact that she couldn't stand the thought of marrying. She wouldn't be able to do it.

If she ever were to take a chance on a man, it would be Ezra. But, no. She wasn't ready to open the lock on all those years of pain. Not now. Not ever.

"It's all right, Tori." Opal's hand squeezed her upper arm with that gentle brush that only her cousin could give. Tori leaned into the feel, letting her eyes drift shut for the smallest of moments.

Then she straightened, exhaling a breath. Now was the time to finish packing, not poke at old wounds she had no intention of ever bringing to light.

Opal tugged at her apron ties and pulled the loop over her head. "I'll go pack my things."

Tori froze, a hundred refusals springing to her lips. She didn't know exactly what the country would be like where she was going. This was different from the stage where they'd had the driver, a shotgun rider, and other passengers to provide protection from unsavory characters. She may well be sleeping on the ground between towns, as she planned to use every bit of daylight she could for travel. It wasn't fair to drag Opal on a journey like that. Not when she finally had a safe place to leave her.

She glanced at Mara, still working the telegraph key across the room. "I think you should stay and help Mara. She'll need assistance with Katie and manning the stage and telegraph, not to mention her own home."

Opal propped a hand on her hip. "Tori, I'm not letting you search the countryside by yourself. I'm going with you."

Panic welled in her chest, but she forced her body to appear calm as she tried to offer a smile to her cousin. "Let's see if Mara finds anything through the telegraph. There may be very little searching required if we locate him." But what condition might he be in if he was holed up in a hotel room somewhere? Shot from another stray bullet? Attacked on the trail and beaten to within an inch of his life?

She couldn't stand the images pulsing through her mind. Turning on her heel, she headed toward Mara for an update on her progress.

As Tori neared, Ezra's sister gasped, even as she scribbled furiously to record an incoming message.

"What is it?" She knew better than to distract her, but the question slipped out before she could stop it.

Thankfully, Mara ignored her, and Tori stood with her hands pressed together, fingers touching her chin. *God, if you love Ezra at all, please keep him safe.* She'd never prayed before, but the words seemed right for this moment. They left her with an odd sense of peace, and she counted her heartbeats as she waited for the clicking to cease.

It wasn't long before Mara straightened, removing her hand from the paper to send the message back for confirmation. Tori strained to read the hurried script.

Ezra Reid ill at Shumeister Boarding House, stop.

That simple sentence started a flurry of hope and fear in Tori's chest that spurred her into action. She ran to the other side of the cabin, grabbing the box of medicines she'd used to tend his bullet wound. She dumped the entire contents into an empty cloth sack, then wound the neck tight so nothing would escape.

Mara had risen and stared at her.

"Mara, where is Shumeister Boarding House? What town did that message come from?" She grabbed the satchel and blankets she'd prepared before, then shifted her load so she could pick up the bag of food Opal had tied neatly closed.

"It's in Mountain Bluff. Josiah and I will go see to him and bring him home."

Tori whirled on her. "You can't travel in your condition. Ezra wouldn't be out there suffering if it weren't for me. Just give me directions, and I'll be on my way."

Mara studied her, and Tori fought the urge to rush her friend. "Ezra will have my head on a silver platter like John the Baptist if I let you go."

"You let me handle your brother." Tori raised her chin. It didn't sound like he would be in a condition to protest, and it was the very least she could do after all he'd done for her. Even after she refused him…

"I'm going with Tori."

Tori whirled on her cousin. "No, you're not. We know where he is, so I won't be searching for him. You'll be of more use helping Mara keep things running here." The feeling of being plotted against sprang up in her chest, almost overwhelming. She grabbed her coat from the peg and opened the door with her foot, since her hands were full.

"I'm going to saddle a horse. Mara, if you could please draw a map or write out directions, I would be most appreciative." And she pulled the door shut before either woman could stop her.

And just at the moment, she didn't care if they disparaged her stubbornness while she was gone.

Ezra needed her. Helping him had to be her focus right now.

CHAPTER 14

Lord, let this be the right town.

Tori slipped her hand inside her saddle bag strapped over the horn, resting her fingers around the grip of the revolver Mara had sent along with her. Something about the cool wood of the handle infused confidence or at least kept the fear from making her tremble.

She'd met so many men on this journey. Or maybe not met them. In South Pass City, she'd spoken only to the clerk and waiters at the hotel and the boy in the livery when she'd dropped off and picked up her horse. Yet every man she passed on the road or the trail seemed to scrutinize her until her skin crawled.

Did every man in the world have a lustful streak as wide as the Sweetwater River, or could that be her imagination? Ezra didn't possess such, and that was why she'd made this harrowing trek. After everything he'd done for her, even offering his name and protection 'til death do them part, the least she could do was come and see he received proper care until he recovered.

Lord, please let him recover. She'd never prayed so much in her life as she had these past two days. In fact, she'd *never* prayed, and she wasn't sure she was doing it right. Did God actually hear these silent pleas of her heart? If she didn't have her head bowed and eyes closed, did the words make it to heaven?

But surely God loved Ezra enough to listen, and each desperate petition left her feeling a little better.

The town seemed more orderly than the last two she'd ridden through, maybe because it was away from the Oregon trail and didn't receive as many visitors as South Pass or Atlantic City.

Even though it must be nearly the dinner hour, the blows of a smithy emanated from the open doors of a building proclaiming itself as a livery. She kept riding, all her weary senses attune to the signs posted on each structure. At last, a blue two-story home caught her eye, well kept with white shutters flanking each of the windows. But it was the sign that brought a surge of panicked relief through her chest.

Shumeister Boarding and Bakery.

How would she find Ezra? Maybe it had only been a heavy cold, and he'd decided to stay on an extra day or two instead of traveling in the frigid weather. Having just made the trip, she could vouch that spending two days in the saddle was not for the faint of heart. But if he were in his right mind at all, surely he would have tried to get a message to them. He would know they'd worry, right? Even if he was still angry with her for refusing his offer, he wouldn't have punished his sister. Not with the clear affection he showed for his family.

After slipping off her horse and tying the mare to the rail, she gathered her nerve and knocked on the door.

It opened to reveal a tall blond man, his somber face decorated with a drooping mustache. "Ja?"

She raised her chin to meet his gaze. "I'm looking for a man named Ezra Reid. I understand he might be here?"

The man stepped aside, opening the door wider to allow her clear entry. "Ja. Herr Reid is here."

She stepped inside, and he closed the door behind her, then turned as if he meant for her to follow. She'd just fallen into step behind him when he paused and turned back to her.

"You are family, ja?" His voice was so heavily accented it took her mind a moment to process each word.

"A friend."

His expression looked uncertain, as though he wasn't sure if she should be admitted. How bad off was Ezra?

"His sister sent me to help him and bring him home."

With a troubled scrunch of his honey-colored brow, the man nodded and turned back toward the stairs.

He scaled them like a mountain goat, and as Tori followed him, her breath came in quick gasps by the time they neared the top. He stopped at the second closed door on the right and tapped a light knock on the door before opening it a gap.

Part of her wanted to peer in over the man's shoulder, but she forced herself to stand quietly. Her lungs struggled to draw air after the climb.

Her host pushed the door wider, then stepped in toward the bed.

As he moved to the side, she was given an unencumbered look at the form shrouded by a field of calico sheets and blankets.

Ezra.

Even though the bedding almost swallowed him, he still seemed strong as she reached his side. His eyelids drifted open, although they looked weighted down, and his gaze seemed unfocused.

"Tori?"

She sank into the chair beside the bed and clasped his hand. "What's wrong, Ezra? What happened?"

His hand was so warm, she looked down at it, wondering anew at how big it was compared to hers. Yet his skin shouldn't be so hot.

"I'm all right."

His words drew her attention back to his face, and she studied every inch of him. A sheen of sweat crossed his forehead. Dark circles under his eyes showed clearly against the unusual pallor of the rest of his skin. She reached to brush the backs of her fingers against his cheek. Definitely too warm.

She turned to the man standing behind her. "I need water and cloths. Have you called a doctor? Has he been drinking water? If you have some willow bark tea, that would help. Or boneset." Opal had gone through a phase several years back where she'd been plagued by fevers, so the process was familiar.

The man nodded. "The doctor is here often." He motioned to the bedside stand where a dark brown bottle and measuring tube sat. "I bring water and my wife make tea."

He turned on his heel and marched out of the room. A man given a task.

She focused on Ezra again. "How did this happen?" She had to know what they were dealing with before she could treat him properly. "Is it an illness or were you injured?"

He motioned toward his arm. "That trifling cut on my arm. Just getting my strength back." But he seemed to struggle with each word, his breath coming in airy gasps. And his eyes seemed to struggle to focus.

"I need to see the arm." He would probably fight this, but if poison had gathered under the scab, it might need to be lanced.

He didn't argue, just pulled that side of the shirt off his shoulder. Apparently, it had been unbuttoned under the sheets, probably to allow the doctor access. The tawny skin of his shoulder molded around lean muscle, and she swallowed hard to keep her mouth from going dry at the sight.

The wound. A loose wrapping of white cloth covered his arm, and she slid it down so she could get a look at the wound. She gasped at the sight of the angry red flesh. A line was cut in the fiery skin, straight enough to be from a scalpel, which meant the doctor must have lanced the infection himself. A decent amount of blood and yellowish substance stained the bandage.

"Here is water."

She straightened at the voice behind her and turned to take the basin and rags from the man. "Thank you. When will the doctor return?" Ezra needed a poultice or something to draw the poison from the wound.

"Dinner."

"Did he leave clean bandages and salve?"

"Bandages there." She glanced up to see him point toward a dresser where a stack of linens rested on top. "Medicine for pain." This time he motioned to the brown bottle on the side table.

She'd have to work with what she had then. First, she dipped a cloth in the water, then wrung it out and smoothed the coolness over Ezra's face.

He groaned a little as she worked, his eyes shut. She continued for several minutes, refreshing the cloth in the cool water several times. At last, his breathing seemed to steady, softer than it had been before.

She set the basin aside and rose. "I'll be right back," she whispered. But hopefully he was relaxed enough he didn't hear her. He needed some tea, and maybe she could find materials for a poultice. Garlic, perhaps. Or black walnut.

After following the sounds of industry down the stairs and through a dining hall, she found an older woman bustling through the kitchen. She was up to her elbows in flour and dough, but motioned toward the kettle on the cook stove when she saw Tori.

"Tea is ready." Her accent was as thick as the man's had been.

As Tori readied a cup for Ezra, she asked about garlic and other supplies for a poultice and was directed to a room off the kitchen. When she opened the door, she discovered a room as full and organized as a dry goods store. Shelves of foodstuffs lined each of the walls, and herbs hung from almost every spot on the ceiling. The woman's pantry was better-stocked than Riverdale's had been.

It took a moment to locate the garlic, and she carried it back to a large work table in the center of the room to slice it in odorous chunks.

"You are his *liebling?*"

Tori looked up at the woman, trying to decipher the words. "Beg your pardon?"

"His treasure. His...how you say? His sweetheart?"

The heat swam up her neck, warming under her collar as she ducked back to focus on her work. "No. Only a friend."

The woman nodded and went back to her work, rolling out dough on another counter. The kitchen was large and well-endowed, from the large cook stove to the multitude of shelves and work surfaces. She must do a good business with the bakery advertised on the sign.

As she finished the poultice and wrapped it in the clean cloth the woman supplied, Tori thanked her and carried a tray of tea and supplies back up the stairs.

Ezra was resting fitfully as she stepped into the room, his head tossing from side to side on the pillow. "Shh... Ezra, it's only me." She placed the tray on the seat she'd occupied before and sank on the edge of the bed.

If she could distract him, it might help ease his discomfort. As she took up the wet cloth again to smooth the sweat from his face, she tried to keep up a steady monologue. "Let's see if we can cool you down for a minute, then I have tea that will make you more comfortable. You need to take in plenty of fluids with your fever so high. And don't worry about whether I've had experience in this before. I've nursed Opal through so many fevers, I could do it with my eyes shut. You're in good hands."

That twitch at the corner of his mouth might have been nothing, but just the thought that it could have been a smile was enough to keep her talking while she continued to wash his face.

"Did I ever tell you in my letters about the time Opal ate so many cherry turnovers she cast up her accounts all over my uncle's front hallway? And then when the doctor was called, she did it again all over his linen trousers. Needless to say, he didn't stick around long that time. And I didn't mind so much if she soiled my clothes."

The ache in her chest pressed hard, and she swallowed down the lump in her throat. She'd dampened Opal's shoulder with tears so many times after Jackson's visits to her room, she'd have done whatever Opal needed to help her recover.

"You and Opal are close." Ezra's voice came through so raspy, and he kept his eyes shut as he spoke.

"Yes. Opal's done so much for me. She's been my dearest friend since I moved in with her family when I was ten. My only friend, really." It was hard to admit that, but she trusted Ezra with the fact. An odd sensation, and the awareness of the trust made the burden in her chest seem to lighten, at least a little.

"What happened to your parents?"

The question caught her up short, and she had to force herself to breathe again. To continue wiping the damp cloth down Ezra's cheek. Had he noticed her pause? He'd seemed almost incoherent from the fever, yet he was able to ask these questions. Did he know their import? Maybe he was just rambling in his fever-induced stupor.

He may not notice if she changed the subject. "Are you ready to drink some tea?"

He answered by parting his lips, but not his eyes. She spooned some in, and he seemed to work at swallowing it, his face wincing with the effort.

"Does your throat hurt?" Maybe it was more than the wound causing his fever. Perhaps he'd also taken ill from a virus.

"Just dry."

She gave him another spoonful of the liquid, and this seemed to go down easier. After two more sips, he let out a breath. Then his eyelids cracked open a sliver. "What happened to your parents?" His voice was stronger this time, more determined. She wouldn't be getting around the question.

So, she met it head on. "They're in prison."

He didn't flinch. Didn't wince. Just kept the tiny beads of his gaze focused on her through the slit of his lashes. "Have you seen them since you were ten?"

She looked down at the tea as she filled the spoon again. "My uncle took me once. My mother cried the entire time, but my father wouldn't speak to me." And that had been the impetus she'd needed to move on. To deal with the fact that her parents had abandoned her. Even if they'd not chosen prison directly, when they began their elaborate swindling operation, they had to know corporal punishment or even death might be a very possible outcome.

Which would leave their daughter defenseless in the hands of her father's brother. A man who could be called negligent at the best of times. In other moods, he could only be described as *cruel*.

Ezra's hand settled on her wrist where she held the cup, his touch callused and much too hot, yet so gentle she had to fight hard against the burn in her eyes.

She lifted the spoon to his mouth with her free hand, and he took the sip. His eyes stayed fixed on her, though. Again, she refilled the spoon and let him drink.

After two more times, he sank back into the pillows, yet still his hand touched her wrist, giving it a gentle squeeze. "I'm sorry things were so hard on you, Tori. I can tell it's made you strong, but if I could take the past away, give you a new history, I would."

His words were more than her defenses could stand, and she dropped her chin as a tear slipped down her cheek.

She had to change the subject, and this time make it stick. "I prepared a garlic poultice for your arm." She set the tea on the side table and gathered up the foul-smelling bundle.

His eyes drifted shut again as she worked to position the wrap around his wound. The fiery skin surrounding the cut had swollen and developed a waxy sheen, and her efforts surely hurt. Yet he didn't cry out.

When she finally had it settled, she pulled the sides of his shirt together across his chest. It was impossible not to admire the breadth of him. Even lying so ill, he sent her pulse into a quick staccato.

She pulled the blanket up to cover his shoulders and couldn't help a final caress to his stubbly cheek. It was almost more than stubble at this point, moving quickly into a full-fledged beard. He probably hadn't shaved since he'd left the Rocky Ridge.

"Thank you." His words were barely more than a whisper, as his chest rose and fell in steady succession.

"See if you can sleep now. I'll be nearby."

His chin bobbed in response.

She eased up from the bed and crept toward the door. Her poor horse needed to be settled at the livery, then she'd be back to Ezra's side until the doctor came.

If he'd had decent care all along, he wouldn't be in this condition now. But at least she could make sure he had everything he needed to recover.

CHAPTER 15

*I*t turned out Mr. Shumeister had already settled her horse at the livery, and her saddle bags were perched at the base of the stairs.

"Here is a tray for your supper and broth for your liebling. I think you want to eat with him, but if you rather take the meal with Mr. Shumeister?" The older woman met Tori with a platter draped by a cloth.

The rich smells that emanated from it brought a gurgle from her middle as she took the heavy tray. "I'll eat upstairs. Thank you."

"Doctor Howard send word he be late tonight. I send him up after he eat dinner."

Tori pinched her mouth shut so nothing slipped out she would regret. Ezra's health was more important than the doctor's stomach, but she could probably tend him as well as the doctor at this point. She nodded. "Thank you."

Ezra seemed to be sleeping as she entered his room, so she settled the tray on the last empty part of the bedside table, then paused to exhale a long breath.

She was so trailworn herself, it would be nice to settle into the room Mrs. Shumeister had said would be hers down the hall. But the aromas wafting from under that cloth on the tray held even more draw. Maybe she could settle for washing her face at the basin on the dresser here in Ezra's room before she inhaled the food.

She stepped around the bed, thankful to see the pitcher was almost full and the basin clean. Splashing cool water over her face awakened her senses, dulling the ache in her head and soothing the tension radiating through her body.

She was here now. Ezra would recover. She hadn't lost him.

After drying her hands on the cloth draped beside the bowl, she turned to take on whatever needed to be done next. Her gaze swept over Ezra, stilling on his face, where wide eyes stared back at her.

Heat flared into her cheeks, although she'd done nothing indecent. Only refreshed herself at the washbasin. Maybe it was the fever that still drooped his eyes, but they seemed to hold a softness. Did that mean he was no longer angry with her for refusing his proposal so adamantly? Or maybe he was too sick to remember.

She tried for a bright smile as she stepped back around the bed toward the tray of food. "Feeling better after a rest?"

"All I've done is rest."

"We're going to get you better now. Think you can eat this broth?" She kept a steady efficiency as she took up the mug and a spoon, then ladled the liquid to his mouth.

He slurped the bite, then sighed as he swallowed. "Good." He took the next sip just as eagerly. "How long have I been sick?"

"I'm not quite sure. We received the telegram that you were ill two days ago, and you'd been gone from the Rocky Ridge four days before that. Do you remember exactly what happened?" She raised another bite to his mouth, trying to focus on the liquid instead of the strong line of his jaw and the even proportion of his lips. The lips she might have been able to kiss had she agreed to his offer.

His shrug pulled her focus away from his face. "Just a little infection. I'm fine. We can start back tomorrow morning."

She sent him a stern frown. "We'll wait until your fever's gone and you're strong enough to travel."

He returned the scowl, pulled his arms out from the covers, and levered his way up to more of a sitting position. "I'm fine, Tori." He reached for the mug of broth. "I'll feed myself."

She started to pull the cup out of his reach, just to show that his orneriness wouldn't work. But the way his hair poked out in spots and the pout of his lips made it easy to imagine how he would have looked as a grumpy five-year-old, giving his mother fits. She relented, handing the mug and spoon to him.

He downed it, alternating between pouring the liquid down his throat and drinking from the spoon. When he finished, he sank back against the pillow with a heavy exhale, handing her the cup. His face had lost some color, except for the red spots appling his cheekbones. Yet his eyes held more light than before.

"I prayed for you." She cupped her hands around the mug, looking down at the cup so she wouldn't have to meet his gaze. She hadn't really meant to say that. "I'm thankful God is healing you."

"I am, too." His warm tone brought her gaze up to his face. "I'm glad you see that He answered your prayer."

She nodded, not really sure what was the proper response. It seemed too much to fathom that God would hear her or care about what she asked of Him. Probably, He answered because her plea had been for Ezra.

"Do you know God loves you, Tori?" His voice was soft, pulling at something deep inside her.

She looked down at the cup again, biting her lip to keep back the sting of tears that threatened to immerge. There was no way he could be right. She'd long since been too stained for love.

"He wants to be there when you need Him. Even more than that, He wants you to be happy. To find joy in Him."

She clutched the mug tighter, willing away the ache that his words brought on. He couldn't be right, but even more than that, she couldn't think about this now. Not in front of him.

"Go get some rest. I'll be ready to leave in the morning."

She looked up at the sudden change of topic, but his eyes had closed. He looked exhausted. Wrung out. "We'll wait until you're better. Rest now."

She squeezed his hand, the contact sending a warmth through her arm. Not necessarily because his skin felt feverish—it seemed closer to normal than it had earlier. No, the warmth of his touch seeped through her in a different way.

For so long now, contact with a man had been a vile thing. Yet Ezra was different. He'd never looked at her as though she were a confection he'd like to consume. Nor had he touched her in any way improper.

Never once had he given her reason to fear him.

And that was proven by the fact that she'd initiated this contact without even thinking about it. And the warmth of it crept to her soul in a way that made her feel protected. Such a very different emotion. Almost frightening in itself.

She pulled away and stood, turning to take the tray that still held her cooling dinner. "I'll leave you to rest."

And give herself time to recover from the realizations coursing through her.

&

"The infection's looking much better."

Tori studied the doctor as they stood at the top of the stairs, speaking in low murmurs after his late-night assessment of Ezra's progress. The man must have been in his late fifties, at least, but the flicker of the lantern in her hands cast deep shadows around his face, turning the age lines into crevices and cliffs. "Have you been giving him something to fight the infection?"

He nodded. "Silver nitrate and another mixture I've concocted. The swelling is less than half the size of when he first took fever three days ago. The redness is lessening, too. I cleaned the wound, but if you want to reapply your poultice in the morning, I don't believe it will do harm."

She stiffened, but maybe this late hour wasn't the time to defend the remedies she'd seen proven effective so many times. After all, the doctor looked so exhausted, he probably wasn't giving proper consideration to any new ideas. If his weariness matched the weight pressing her own shoulders, she should let him sleep.

Nodding, she said. "Thank you, doctor. I'll stay by his bed tonight should he need anything. Will you be in to check him in the morning?"

"I will, but you don't need to lose sleep tonight. He's much recovered and shouldn't need to be supervised constantly. Sleep in the room Mrs. S prepared for you. I'll look in on him before I leave for calls in the morning."

He turned and trudged down the hallway, fading into the darkness outside the scope of her lantern. A click sounded as a door opened, then another as it closed. It was surely a good thing to have the doctor under the same roof in case Ezra needed him suddenly.

She crept toward the closed door to Ezra's room, then turned the knob as quietly as she could. The regular sound of his breathing drifted through the dim chamber, and she stood looking into the darkness. Relishing the steady noise.

Should she sleep in the chair in case his fever took a turn for the worse? She stepped into the room, keeping her tread as soft as her boots would allow. But Ezra stirred, pausing her mid-stride. The room Mrs. Shumeister had assigned her was next door, so maybe that would be close enough. Especially if she rose to check on him several times through the night.

Barely daring to breathe, she crept backward and eased the door closed. Even through the wood panel, the sound of his steady breathing drifted to her, calming the unease in her chest. Sleep would help him as much as anything at this point.

～

*S*tay until Ezra is well, stop. Josiah can come if needed, stop.

Tori smiled at the telegraph the messenger had just delivered. The operator hadn't been able to get a message through to Mara until this morning, but she'd been quick to respond.

And she needn't worry about Tori rushing their return trip. She had no desire to travel that terrain again without an able-bodied partner beside her. Even though she could hit what she aimed at if it were close enough, but there was strength in numbers. And this was a comfortable place for Ezra to recover. Especially with the aromas of sweet breads and spicy sausages drifting up from the kitchen all morning. She needed to go down and offer to help their host, but Ezra still seemed so weak, she hated to leave his side for long. At least his fever seemed to have broken.

She lowered the paper to her lap and smiled at the man who'd become the constant center of her thoughts these days.

"Is it good news?" His voice graveled like it had been dragged across a washboard.

She handed the message over, watching him take in the two lines with a scan of his gaze. He sank back against the pillow and let his hand holding the paper drop to the blanket. "She's always worried."

"I think that's what big sisters are supposed to do."

He raised a tired brow. "I may have needed it when I was little, but I'm a big fellow now. I love my sister, but she can be a bit over-concerned at times. She has enough to worry about with her own growing family."

Tori smiled. "It's exciting, isn't it? The thought of a baby." Too bad she wouldn't be around when the time came.

He answered her smile with a curve of his mouth, but it didn't hold the life a smile should. "Yes." And then, as though he'd followed her line of thought, his face lost all pretense of pleasure. "I've found work that seems a good fit for you and Opal."

The words sent a piercing knife through her chest, stealing her breath as though they punctured a lung. "You...did? Where?" She sank back against the chair.

His face looked so worn, yet a resolve had touched his eyes. "Here."

"Here?" The meaning seemed to have trouble penetrating her mind.

He nodded, and the Adam's apple at his throat bobbed. "Mrs. Shumeister needs help with the bakery. They'll give you each room and board, along with a dollar a week. It's a fair deal, and this seems like a quiet town." His throat worked again.

A shadow had covered his eyes, and he seemed to be studying her. Probably waiting for her response. But she had none.

She should thank him. He'd worked so hard to find exactly what they'd asked for. Yet this place was so far from the Rocky Ridge. Two days' ride was no small distance. She pinched one of the trailing flowers on her heavy muslin skirt. Would she ever see him again if they took this job?

"It makes sense for you to stay here now. I'll ride back and retrieve Opal, then bring her to join you."

She jerked her head up. "Stay now?" She had no power to contain the squeak in her voice.

He nodded, but his eyes were so hooded she still couldn't read his thoughts. Did he want to be rid of her? Of course he did. She'd been nothing but work for him. Showing up on his doorstep and inter-rupting the life he'd planned. If he'd not been out searching on their behalf, he never would have received this gunshot wound in the first place. And when he'd come up with a viable option for a comfortable home for her and Opal, she'd turned him down immediately. A deci-sion she was coming to regret.

If she'd said yes, would she now be this man's wife? Her wayward gaze traveled across his face, flicking down to the strong expanse of his shoulders before dropping to her hands. Was there any chance he would ask her again? What man would propose a second time after being refused? Especially when he'd not even loved her to begin with.

But what was she thinking? She stiffened her spine, squaring her shoulders. She didn't want him to ask again. She'd decided long ago she'd never marry, decided it the first time her innocence had been stolen.

She had to stand strong now, especially since her and Opal's goal was in sight. Forcing herself to meet Ezra's gaze, she nodded. "All right."

CHAPTER 16

*E*zra fought through the weakness in his muscles and kept his gelding moving on the trail.

Almost home now. The prospect should thrill him, since he'd been gone well over a week. But with every hour in the saddle, his insides seemed to shrivel tighter until he had almost no emotion left.

And his mind wasn't much better. All he could think of was the picture of Tori as she stood on the boardwalk in front of the boarding house, watching him ride away. A statue amidst the flurry of turmoil roiling in his chest.

How could he have left her there?

Yet how could he do anything else? She'd already said she'd never marry him. That he wasn't enough to change her plans. So he'd helped her accomplish them. The Shumeisters's home in the little town of Mountain Peak was by far the best arrangement he'd found for the women. Maybe the fact that he wouldn't be around to protect them was what ate at his peace of mind.

He was fooling himself with that line of thinking.

He hadn't seen it coming, but he was pretty sure he knew what was causing the powerful ache in his chest. He loved Tori Reid.

So, the question now…what was he going to do about it?

~

*T*hat look on Mara's face spelled trouble every time. And usually the ruckus came in the form of meddling, so Ezra steeled himself as she stomped across the muddy courtyard.

When she neared, he thrust Jack's lead rope toward her. "Here, walk this boy while I get Jim."

She accepted the line and held her tongue as he turned back to the pasture gate to retrieve the other gelding. But the burn of her gaze was strong enough he didn't need his coat, despite the fact he could see his breath cloud in front of him. Josiah had brought Mara, Opal, and Katie over first thing that morning, and he and Opal would be heading out shortly with the buckboard. Hitting the trail toward Mountain Pass.

He still hadn't decided what to do about Tori, but he had promised her that he'd bring Opal to her. He was keeping that promise. If nothing else, it was one more opportunity to see Tori before a final goodbye. Maybe they'd have a chance to talk while he was there. He could test the waters and see if she might be willing to change her answer.

If she'd been through what he was imagining in her young life, he didn't blame her for not wanting anything to do with men. Would it make any difference if he told her how much he'd come to love her? Probably not. If anything, that would likely scare her away.

If the offer of a chaste marriage didn't sway her, probably nothing would. And in a strange way, he was almost glad she'd declined that particular proposition. There was a good chance he wouldn't have been able to follow through with his promise. No, Tori Boyd had the power to light fire in his veins. It took a lot of work to keep the coals banked every time she came near.

With Jim's rope in hand and the gate latch refastened, he turned back toward the barn. And his sister.

"You're being a coward, Ezra Michael. You know that, right?"

He steeled his jaw, not giving her the acknowledgement of even a glance. If he waited, she'd soon tell him why he'd caught her ire this time.

But his stubborn sister didn't speak again. Not as they led the horses into the barn and tied them off. Nor as they fastened the double harness onto the geldings.

The silence stretched heavy as she handed straps across Jack's back, eyeing him with a look equal parts exasperated and disappointed.

At last, he straightened and glared at her. "What, Mara? What have I done to disappoint you this time?"

Her gaze softened, and he had the sense that if the two horses hadn't stood between them, she would have reached out and hugged him. She had the ability to get sentimental like that. Thank the Lord for Jim and Jack.

"You don't disappoint me, Ezra. But I'm afraid you're going to let your fear or pride—or whatever it is—hold you back from the best thing that could ever happen to you."

"And what's the best thing that could happen to me?" He couldn't help the sour tone. Didn't he have enough on his mind without Mara coming to direct his life in one more area? He was twenty-six years old, for land sakes. He could make his own decisions.

"Tori."

He couldn't stop the wince at her name, so he moved to the horses' heads to lead them to the buckboard. "Leave it alone, Mara. Tori is finally where she needs to be, and Opal will be there, too, in a couple of days."

And what exactly did his sister want from him? He could tell by the look in her eyes and her tone that she was attempting a bit of cupid's work, but they'd never discussed how he felt about the woman. He'd not even told her he'd offered marriage—and been heartily declined.

Maybe Tori had told her.

Regardless, this wasn't Mara's bone to chew. As he pulled the horses to a stop in front of the wagon, he squared his shoulders and turned to face his sister, who'd dogged his heels with every step. "Let me be clear, sister. I've made my decision. And Tori has made hers. This is none of your affair."

She studied him, concern slanting her eyes in the sunlight. Then she reached to place her hand on his forearm. "You're always my affair. But I forget sometimes that you're all grown up now. I won't interfere, Ezra. But I do want to say one thing."

A smile crept to his mouth, unbidden and completely unwanted. She couldn't keep from meddling to save her very soul. But that love and caring was what made her special. The best big sister a fellow could have. Usually.

"Don't be afraid to step out in faith. Your heart will tell you when the time is right, even if your mind tells you it's not safe." She smiled at him, her wet eyes shimmering in the brightness.

He wrapped an arm around her shoulders and pulled her to his side. "Thanks. You're not so bad for a sister, even when you meddle."

She sniffed and squeezed him back. "I'm the second-best thing that's ever happened to you."

He chuckled. But he wasn't about to touch that one.

~

"*B*ut you can't leave, liebling."

Tori dropped her satchel to the floor and turned to face the older woman, who'd been trailing her to the front door.

Mrs. Shumeister stood there, clutching the cloth bundle she'd prepared, the lines of her well-padded face drooping as though she were sending her only child away to war.

"I think this is what I need to do, although if it doesn't work out, I'll be back on your doorstep." She tried to summon a smile through the butterflies in her stomach. In just a few days of working beside her in the kitchen, Mrs. S. had become a dear friend. Though her quiet efficiency came across as brusqueness at first meeting, the woman had a generous and loving soul.

Tori stepped forward to take the bundle of baked tasties from her grip. On impulse, she reached to squeeze one of the fleshy hands to show her thankfulness. Touch, as an expression of kindness, was still a hard concept for her body to accept, but she was trying.

Mrs. S. turned her hand so she took Tori's into her own with a squeeze, then she gave a tug and pulled Tori into a full embrace.

The shock of the contact almost made her jerk back, but she stilled her reflexes, trying to relax as the familiar scents of yeast and flour filled her nose.

"*Gott sei mit dir.*" Mrs. S. squeezed tight. "God be with you."

A strong burn crowded Tori's eyes as she breathed in the love in the woman's touch. "Thank you." She couldn't remember ever being hugged by her mother, but she imagined it would have felt like this.

After a moment, she eased back and gripped each of the woman's hands. "Even if I don't come back to stay, I promise I'll visit. Thank you for all you've done. For me and for Ezra."

Mrs. S. nodded, looking down as though embarrassed by her display of emotion.

Tori turned away. "Please give Mr. S. my thanks, too."

"Ja. I will."

With emotions churning inside her, Tori stepped outside. Maybe she was making a mistake, but she just couldn't stomach the thought of giving Ezra up. If she had to put a name to the longing that almost squeezed the breath from her, she would have to call it love. As terrifying as that thought might be, the prospect of losing him forever was more than she was ready to face.

Hopefully, she could reach the Rocky Ridge before he started his return journey with Opal. She would tell him she'd changed her mind. Should she tell him anything more? He would probably be able to read it all over her face. Maybe. She could decide the extent of the conversation later.

For now, she had to traverse the two days' ride through the wilderness on her own.

Again.

❧

*T*he land stretched before Tori, the river snaking in the distance. Finally, she'd made her way through the most treacherous of the mountainous country, meeting up with what they called the Oregon Trail. The sun had long since reached its apex and descended, so that the mountains in the west hid the strongest of the rays. A chilly wind whipped around her, slipping under the neckline of her coat and sending cold bumps down her arms.

Another few hours, then she'd find a copse of trees off the trail and make camp for the night. She'd left Mountain Bluff too late this morning to make it all the way to South Pass City before night fell. But tomorrow, she'd ride through South Pass and Atlantic Cities, then hopefully arrive at the Rocky Ridge before dark.

Ezra would have arrived home two days before, but hopefully he'd decided to wait a few days before making the return trip.

His body was stronger, but he hadn't quite regained his full vigor.

Her mare's ears pricked, drawing Tori's attention as the horse studied the far tree line. A thudding sounded in the distance, and an object separated from the brown of the woods.

A coach, and from the speed they traveled, it was likely the westbound stage. She nudged her mare forward as she watched the approaching rig.

The details of the horses and coach became distinct, and she studied the two figures on the driver's bench. One wore the buckskins many drivers and guards seemed to prefer, while the man holding the rifle looked to be in the standard wool shirt and lapel coat of a working-class man.

Neither looked familiar, which was to be expected, since this stretch of the line would be manned by a different relay team than those who serviced the stretch near the Rocky Ridge.

Still, she raised a hand in greeting as she reined her horse to the side of the road for the Concorde coach to pass. Both men in the front returned the greeting, although the coach barely slowed.

The inside shades were lowered except for one window. A man's arm covered in the dark wool of a coat and black leather gloves rested across the sill. It was likely cold inside, with nothing to pass the time except gripping the seat to keep from lurching to the floor. Yet something about that glove sent a finger of dread through her. Jackson had worn a pair just like that when he called on the farmers working the Riverdale land. Yet, black leather gloves must be as common as a cravat in every gentleman's wardrobe—even those who only pretended to be gentlemen. She forced herself to take even breaths as the coach passed.

Two horses trailed the vehicle on long tethers, a practice she'd seen occasionally with the stages at the Rocky Ridge. Their riders must have thought the trip would be more comfortable by coach, or at least more expedient. She always felt sorry for those trailing horses, though. They didn't have a way to voice when they became too exhausted by the steady run. The coach horses were changed out at regular intervals, but these animals had to endure the entire journey. Hopefully it would be a short one for this pair of mounts.

Within moments, the coach was gone. Nothing more than a rumble behind her as she pushed on.

She stopped for the night as the dusky light of evening settled over the landscape. By the time she found a spot to camp a little way into the woods, the darkness seemed to be coming more quickly. She tied her mare to a sapling, then hurried to build a fire. Mrs. S. had sent a box of fresh matches, so it didn't take long to get the small wood burning. Most of the larger pieces she found were wet from the recent snows, but she was able to find enough dry wood beneath the top layer of bracken to build the blaze. Once she got it going, she propped several pieces around the perimeter of the fire so the heat could help dry them for use through the night.

The warmth was beginning to thaw her extremities now, and she needed to settle her mare for the night. But the gnawing in her belly had spread to a pounding in her head. She'd gone too long without food today, so it might be best if she ate a little from the bundle Mrs. S. had prepared, then she could finish making camp.

She removed her gloves to open the cloth bundle, then reached for one of the sausages rolled in a flaky bread blanket. The dish had looked appealing at lunch, but she'd chosen the cheese-filled dumplings instead. The way the woman infused each food with so many intense flavors set her taste buds to tingling.

These wrapped sausages were no different. Her eyelids sank closed as the flavors spread through her mouth. The stomp of her mare's hoof behind her barely registered as her stomach gurgled its eagerness for the treat. But the sausage was so rich, her mouth begged to relish the taste a little longer.

Something solid struck her cheek, and she squealed as it closed over her lips, jerking her from her revelry.

A hand. And another gripping around the front of her, locking her arms to her side.

She tried to scream, but the flesh clamped over her mouth concealed all sound.

CHAPTER 17

$\mathcal{T}$ori fought back, the terror of being cinched in the grasp of a strange man. Her shrieks couldn't escape his hand over her jaws, but the food tumbling in her mouth hit her throat with a gag. She convulsed, trying to expel the food and the almost-paralyzing fear that shrouded her, hemming her in as much as the brutish arms clamping her tight.

Voices sounded around her, and she struggled to clear her mind enough to listen. But the old familiar desperation pressed down on her shoulders. Forced the air from her lungs. She wouldn't be able to escape him. It would go better for her if she submitted. And if she closed her eyes and found that other place, she could get away from this reality, at least in her mind.

That place called to her, but she forced the image back. Forced herself to open her eyes. The blackness of the night was as thick as a murky swamp, but gradually the light from the fire penetrated her awareness.

A voice spoke again, the deep rumble of a man. Close enough to her ear it was probably the brute who held her captive. She fought against a tremble, clamping her jaw to strengthen her defenses.

"...doubt she would have left the chit alone. Let's see what she has to say on the matter."

That voice. She couldn't stop the shaking now, springing from her core and taking over the whole of her.

He couldn't be here. She must be imagining him as part of this nightmare.

A motion at the corner of her vision pulled her focus, and the shadows from the shifting firelight made it hard to focus. The form of a man took shape, coming to stand in front of her so that she had to crane her neck up to look at him.

The other beast still had his hand over her mouth, but he eased it enough for her to lift her chin.

"My dear, Victoria. I've missed you."

With the sound of her name in his nasally tone, the shaking stilled. Replaced by a raw fury.

How dare this man follow her thousands of miles? Did the extent of his wicked fascination have no bounds? It wasn't enough that he'd stripped her of her innocence, using her body in vile and unspeakable ways through the years, then attempted to do the same with Opal after Tori finally escaped his hold.

But now that she'd rescued Opal from the man. Now that they both had a chance at...well, if not happiness, at least freedom from his particular brand of torment.

Now, he thought to chase them thousands of miles to regain what he'd lost?

A pox on the man. She gathered spit in her mouth, but the grubby paw blocked her from fulfilling the impulse.

"I see you've missed me, too, darling."

She inhaled a deep breath through her nose as the anger boiled inside her. The air was laced with the hefty stench of dirt and sweat and something that smelled like dung, sending her stomach roiling in her throat. It would do the man good if she cast up her accounts all over him.

But no. She needed to be in complete control of herself just now. These men may have brute strength, but they no longer enjoyed the advantage of surprise. And they certainly didn't have the benefit of intellectual superiority.

Still, it would take all her focus to find a way out of this.

"Where's your sniveling cousin?"

The grubby hand lowered from her mouth, sliding down to her neck and tightening against her voicebox.

She raised her chin and glared at Jackson. Thankfully, with the fire angled slightly behind him, she could see only his outline. At least she didn't have to look at his despicable face.

"I never liked her as much as you, my dear. You have a certain… strength…that she lacks. A feral tendency that I find most alluring."

This time she did spit at him, although in the darkness she couldn't see his reaction.

But his chuckle filled the cold night. Mirthless, sending another burst of fury through her. She hated this man with every fiber of her being.

"Don't worry, Victoria. You and I will have our time of reunion. But first, I need your help. Your uncle has tasked me with finding his daughter and returning her home safely." He stepped nearer, stopping less than a foot away. The smells of his pomade and cologne water wafted through her senses, and her body revolted against the memories the odors elicited. Her mind began to shut down, and she saw herself as though looking from the outside, from a distance.

No. She had to remain present for this. Had to best the snake this time.

He touched her chin, tipping it up so she had to face him fully. She fought against the urge to slink away. Fought against the urge to distance herself. Fought to keep down the bile churning into her throat.

"Where is she?" His voice had lost all its syrupy sweetness, condensing into a sharp bite of anger.

She clamped her jaw.

The grubby hands at her throat tightened, restricting part of her airflow. She forced herself not to show the fear welling in her chest. This leech fed on fear and would pounce at the first sign.

His finger followed the edge of her jaw, trailing to her ear, stroking the sensitive skin behind it. She clamped tighter to keep from biting at him. The vise closing her throat helped keep her steady.

His hand moved to her shoulder, pressing firmly enough that she could feel every finger through the thickness of her coat. And then he was tugging at the collar, pulling the buttons, igniting terror in her chest.

God, help. The prayer exploded in her mind, and she hoped he couldn't see her eyes squeeze shut. *Save me.* She may not be worth His notice, but maybe…just maybe…Ezra was right.

Even if God didn't care whether she was happy…if he would just keep her from this evil. *God, I can't do this again. Please. Save me.*

Down the front of her coat, she could feel the buttons release. Jackson worked in slow precision. She kept her eyes shut. Looking at his vile image just inches from her would be more than she could stand. Just feeling his breath on her face and the skin now exposed below her neck was almost enough to push her over the brink into that other place.

God, help me. She repeated the cry over and over until the prayer seared itself in her mind.

And then a blast rent the night air, jolting her heart into her throat. The hands at her neck loosened as a curse filled the ensuing silence.

"Tie her up. I'll see what's happening." Jackson's voice rumbled, then the leaves rustled as he disappeared.

Even as the brute man-handled her into an awkward position face down in the forest floor, her ears strained to hear more sounds from the direction of the gunfire. A hunter maybe? Or had someone heard them?

No matter the reason, God had given her a reprieve—at least for the moment—from Jackson's attention. Now she could find a way of escape.

God, show me.

Her captor had jerked the leather cord tight enough to restrict her blood flow by the time a rustle of leaves signaled the approach of another person. She fought the urge to crane her neck and see, but she could still feel the imprints of the thug's hands around her throat, and the last thing she wanted to do was bring his attention back to her.

"I think it was just a hunter. Saw a man hunched over a deer. But we need to get out of here." Jackson's voice.

More shuffling sounded behind her, then the low nicker of a horse. Her mare? Maybe. Where were they going and did they plan to take her?

Then without warning, she was hoisted up by her arms and tossed into the air. She landed with a thud on the man's thick shoulder. The blow to her middle almost knocked the breath from her, and she panted to regain her balance. Not an easy thing when she was practically draped upside down.

The man grunted and carried her several steps, then lifted her again and held her suspended in front of him. "Put your leg over."

If this was what a rag doll felt like, she now had great sympathy for the cloth moppet Opal had carried around when they were still in short skirts. She gritted her teeth against the man's fingers digging into her ribs and stretched her right leg up over the horse's rump.

He shoved her upright behind a tall lean form, and a new wave of pomade washed through her senses. She leaned backward to create as much space as possible between Jackson's back and herself. Yet with her hands tied behind her, she'd have to find something to grip to keep herself on the horse when they started moving.

Or maybe she should let herself fall off the back of the animal. Would they notice she was gone? She could be injured in the fall, but probably only a temporary physical pain, nothing like the damage Jackson would inflict when he got her alone.

~

"*Ho*." Ezra reined the team to a stop in front of the hotel, then set the brake on the buckboard and jumped down to help Opal climb up to the bench. They'd left the stage station late the morning before and made it as far as South Pass City. The horses shuffled their impatience, fresh after a night in the livery.

Once Opal was settled on the seat, he strode around the team and climbed to his own spot. He flicked the reins and the horses stepped out. The wagon moved slower than horseback, and they would have to spend a second night on the trail anyway, so he'd opted to take three days to travel and spend the first night in this final town before heading out into the foothills of the Rockies.

Opal had remained so quiet yesterday, and he still couldn't get a read on whether she was nervous spending this much time alone with him or whether she just enjoyed the silence. He wanted her to be comfortable, but he sure didn't mind the lack of gab.

They made their way out of town and settled into an easy rhythm on the rutted Oregon Trail. Not many travelers were out this morning, and the air had a crisp bite to it, even through his buckskins.

He glanced sideways at his passenger. She curled her gloved hands around each other, as if trying to keep her fingers warm.

"I tucked the furs under the seat if you get cold."

She reached under her skirts and pulled out the buffalo hide, then spread it over herself, offering one end to him.

He waved it off. "I'm fine for now."

One of the horses issued a shrill whinny, grabbing Ezra's attention. An answering nicker sounded from a copse of trees to their right, its tone high and quick as if the horse were excited.

He tightened his hold on the reins as Jim and Jack raised heads high toward the sound, tails flagging.

A horse cantered from the trees, saddled but without a rider, loose reins flapping with each stride. The animal was a dappled gray mare that took him a moment to place. If he wasn't mistaken, this was one of Josiah's three-year-old mares that Tori sometimes rode when she came over to the Rocky Ridge. The last time he'd seen those wide-set eyes and that funny cockeyed blaze was in the livery in Mountain Bluff.

A cold fear gripped his muscles, and he jerked his team to a halt, then thrust the reins at Opal. After jumping to the ground, he jogged toward the horse but forced himself to slow when the skittish animal shied away from him.

"Hey, girl. It's all right. Where's Tori?" He tried to find a crooning tone and held out his hand, advancing at a slower walk.

He was within a few strides of the horse, but the animal looked like it was torn between investigating what might be in his outstretched hand and bolting down the trail. Leaves and twigs littered its mane and back, and the saddle was askew, as though she'd been wearing it a while. This was definitely the mare from Josiah's ranch. Only one horse could have both the unusual face marking *and* the splash of white in a band just above her left front hoof, stretching much higher on the inside than the outside.

So where was Tori? How had her horse traveled so far? This was at least a hard day's ride away from the Mountain Bluff.

The mare allowed him to close the distance and grasp a rein. He stroked her neck, as much to calm her quivering muscles as to reward her for letting him approach. "Where's Tori, girl?"

The horse blew into his hand, then dipped her head as he rubbed up her flat forehead.

"Can you take me to her?"

His heartbeat pulsed through his chest as he turned and strode back to the wagon, the horse plodding behind him. It seemed almost relieved to have been caught.

"Whose horse is it?" Opal's face was a mask of concern as he strode past her to tie the animal to the rear of the wagon.

He didn't answer right away, but finished his task, then made his way back around the wagon so he stood beside Opal. "It's the horse Tori rode to Mountain Bluff."

Her face blanched. "How did it get out here? Is she hurt?"

"She must have left there for some reason, probably coming back home." He scrubbed a hand through his hair. "Although why she would risk traveling that distance alone—a second time—boggles the mind." And it lit a fire inside him. Her impetuous tendencies were going to get her hurt one day. *Please, God, don't let this be the day.*

CHAPTER 18

$\mathcal{E}$zra had to focus. His mind spun with what to do as he looked up at Opal, shielding his eyes against the glare of the morning sun. "Can you manage the wagon? I'm going into the woods to see if I can follow her horse's trail. The animal came from the trees, but I'm thinking she must have been riding the Oregon Trail. Once I find where she left it, I'll either call for you or come back to get you."

She nodded. "Of course."

He set off at a jog, entering the woods in the spot he'd seen the horse leave. Her trail wasn't hard to follow, since the horse had been running pell-mell, churning leaves and snapping branches as it went.

He followed the winding trail as it moved mostly westward. After about ten minutes of trotting along the path, he veered left toward the edge of the woods and called for Opal to drive the team forward.

"Stay on the road for another five minutes or so. I think the horse's tracks will keep moving parallel to the main trail."

She nodded, then snapped the reins and called for the team to walk on.

For a quarter hour at least, they proceeded in that manner. And then the woods ended in a rocky bluff, but he was able to pick out the deep hoof marks pressed into the ground amongst the stones around the base of the cliff.

Then the woods began again, and he followed the same set of fresh tracks into the shadows. It was interesting that the horse had stayed in the forest instead of moving to the open road.

Opal kept the team driving at about the same pace he traveled, as he was able to jog through much of the way. His breath was coming in deep pants now, probably as much from the steady run as from the race of his pulse.

His mind tried to wander through all the possible scenarios as to why Tori's horse would be running through the wilderness, riderless and obviously frightened. But he couldn't let his thoughts conjure images. He had to focus on picking up all the signs the trail might hold for him.

As he jogged through the woods, dodging trees, a cedar sapling caught his notice. Several bare spots showed in the trunk where twigs had been snapped from it, and the dead needles at the base had been stirred into a frenzy. Hoof prints marred the mud where the forest residue had been pawed away.

And then he saw the ashes from a campfire, the flattened area where someone must have sat. The churned leaves around that circle.

He stepped closer. Maybe he could distinguish Tori's lady-sized boot prints. Although, from the amount of activity the ground showed, she'd either been here a while, or there was more than one person.

A glimmer of gold caught in the light filtering through the trees. He bent down and picked up a finely braided gold chain necklace, with a pendant shaped in the outline of a heart, no bigger than the pad of his little finger.

Was it Tori's? It certainly belonged to a woman, but he couldn't say he'd ever seen her wear jewelry. Opal would know for sure.

He turned and sprinted toward the road.

When he reached the wagon, he had to fight to draw enough breath to speak. So he held up the necklace without a word.

Opal's face paled and she reached for the pendant and took it from him.

"Is it...hers?" He forced out the words through his parched throat.

"I gave it to her on her eighteenth birthday. To celebrate her freedom." Opal's distressed gaze flew to his face. "What's happened?"

He shook his head, fighting against the bile churning in his gut. "I found where she must have camped. It looks like tracks go three ways, at least one of them headed north toward the mountains. I'm going to start that way. Do you think you can take the team back to South Pass and wait for me there?"

She stiffened. "I'm coming, too. Maybe I can follow one of the other trails." She started to set the wagon's brake, but she was such a willowy thing, it required her entire body to complete the action.

Could he let her come with him? She'd be so much safer tucked back in the hotel in South Pass City. But if she had any of Tori's stubborn streak running through her, he'd waste too much time trying to talk her out of accompanying him. And at least this way, he'd be there to keep her safe. Besides, maybe she would have insight into where Tori might have gone.

"Loosen that brake again. We'll move the wagon to the trees, then unhitch the horses and settle them. I think they'll be safe enough there. Hopefully we won't be gone long." *Lord, let us find her soon.* He tried not to show the fear surging through his veins.

Opal worked with quick efficiency while they settled the team. She was usually competent, but in a mild, almost invisible way. Getting things done without you realizing she was doing them. Right now, she worked as a woman intent on her purpose, taking over the team from him with a brusque determination. "I'll do this." Her voice held an undertone of steel.

He nodded. "We'll take Tori's mare. We can pack supplies in the saddle bags, and you'll ride her.

Even with them working together, it seemed like hours before they had Jim and Jack settled and Opal mounted on the gray. Finally, Ezra checked the pistol he'd tucked in his waistband, then set off on foot, Opal's horse trailing him.

When they reached Tori's empty campsite, he inspected the ground again to catch anything he'd been too distressed to see before. He found small boot prints in a section of muddy moss that must have been from Tori. And there were several places where horse hooves had dug into the leaves to uncover mulch and mud underneath, as though they'd been pawing while they were tied.

Then he checked the tracks leading away from the area. The one set was, of course, the trail he'd been following from Tori's horse when it fled the scene. And another single set of horse prints led from a southwesterly direction, as if it had been tracking from the road. Maybe Tori had been riding the Oregon Trail and come into the woods to camp? That made sense.

So the only trail unexplained was the more heavily traveled tracks heading north. Into the mountains.

They headed that way, and at first, he studied each print, trying to reconstruct who had traveled this direction and how. Every time his mind wandered to the why, it almost paralyzed his thoughts.

He pushed faster, no longer analyzing each track, but making sure he stayed on their trail. Whatever had happened to Tori, she needed help now. He had to find her.

The trees began to thin, strengthening the daylight around them. Yet the sun's rays had dimmed behind a blanket of low, gray clouds. The air had grown even colder than when they'd started that morning, and it burned his lungs as he took deep gulps to fuel his hike. Finally, the woods opened into a rocky country, with stone bluffs scattered across their view.

He paused to take in the scene. No evidence of people marred the wilderness, and the rocky ground might make it harder to follow Tori's tracks.

Something wet touched his nose and he swiped at it as he looked up.

"It's snowing." Opal spoke the words that had formed in his mind.

He glanced at her, the implication of this new development taking shape in his mind. Snow would make it almost impossible to follow

Tori's trail. And if she weren't prepared for the elements, she could freeze to death before they reached her.

Oh, God. They had to find Tori. Now.

~

*T*he farther they rode into the mountain wilderness, the more Tori's body tried to retreat to the place where she no longer had to feel or see or know. She could block out the way her legs occasionally brushed against Jackson as the horse jostled, climbing rocky hills and trekking down steep inclines. Riding behind his saddle, with her hands tied behind her back, it was a wonder she didn't slide off completely. Only the vise grip she clutched on the saddle blanket kept her in place.

They'd rode several hours in the night, then the men made camp. They'd kept her tied to a tree, albeit in a position where she could have shifted around to lie on her side, her hands still strapped behind her. It wouldn't have been comfortable, but she may have slept if she'd wanted to. But sleep was the last thing she'd attempt with these vultures so close. Yet, by the grace of God, they'd ignored her.

Even this morning, after the two had slept hours past sunrise, then cooked a hot breakfast over the fire, they'd not given her the time of day. They barely even spoke to each other. When Jackson disappeared around a cluster of boulders, the big man had offered her a flapjack and piece of jerked meat. Her stomach had churned when he pushed the food in her mouth with his grubby hands, but she had to keep her strength up if she was going to get away from these despoilers.

And now, they'd been back on the trail for at least a couple more hours. Where were they taking her? These men rode as if they had a purpose and knew their destination exactly. Jackson wouldn't be familiar with this country, she was fairly certain. As far as she knew, he'd not left Pennsylvania these last ten years, at least. And he'd never seemed like the type to explore the wilderness for pleasure.

So was the other man a local? He was a big, beefy fellow, wrapped in a buckskin coat with a beard covering most of his face. He certainly looked like he could be accustomed to life in these western mountains. Did he have a cabin out here? If Jackson had been sent to find Opal, why didn't he pressure her again for answers?

She was more than thankful he hadn't pressed his advantage again, but the farther they strayed from the main road, the harder it would be for her to find help when she escaped.

And she *would* escape. She had to hold onto that determination.

Snowflakes had been pricking her face in occasional flurries, but now fell in steady succession. She hadn't been able to feel her hands for several hours, except where the rough blanket burned her fingers as she gripped it. Not even the warmth from the horse's back penetrated her numbness.

They rode farther as the snow fell in a thick haze. The hours seemed to blur, and she huddled into herself. It didn't even matter so much if her body brushed against her captor, solid in the saddle in front of her. The cold had taken a chokehold on her and stripped away anything except the desire for warmth.

And even that desire no longer seemed so important. She just wanted it to end. Wanted everything to end. Exhaustion seeped through her almost as intensely as the cold, and she pressed her eyes shut. *God, if you have any pity, take me now.*

This life was too hard. Nothing had ever been easy. Nothing good since her parents had chosen their selfish thievery over her well-being. Nothing good except Opal.

An image of her cousin slipped through her mind, standing at the stove in Ezra's cabin. The picture in her memory shifted to Ezra himself, perched at the kitchen table. His arms were draped across the table as he leaned forward, and he seemed to be staring at her. Or… maybe he was speaking to her. She struggled to hear him.

"Do you know God loves you, Tori?" His soft voice held an intensity which seemed to pierce her along with his gaze. "He wants to be there when you need Him. Even more than that, He wants you to be happy. To find joy in Him."

She struggled to take in the words. They didn't cut deep like they once had. Because he'd said them before. She couldn't remember when, but this time they soaked through her, and she clung to them. "I need Him now, Ezra, but I don't know how to find Him." She tried to speak the words, but her mouth wouldn't work.

He must have understood, though, because he answered. "Just say His name, and He'll be there. All you have to do is ask."

"You mean...Jesus?"

Ezra nodded, but he seemed to grow blurry in her vision. The entire cabin dimmed, and she struggled to focus. "Ezra?"

Just say His name. The words were like a whisper in her heart.

Jesus. Jesus, help me. The warmth that had seemed to reach out to her from the cabin faded, and the chill of the mountains crept in to brush against her cheeks. Yet the cold didn't penetrate any deeper.

Jesus. The name echoed in her mind, and with each reverberation, her senses came back to life. Awareness crept into her thoughts as surely as her fingers resurrected with aching intensity.

Her head bumped against something, and she straightened, unfolding herself from where she'd curled into a ball. The top of her head must have been pressed against the back of the man in front of her.

Jackson.

She stiffened, the full extent of her situation flooding back like a crashing wave that jolted her awake.

Mountains crested high around her, and snow fell in a steady cascade. When would they stop? Where were they going? Maybe she could ask, although the thought of initiating conversation with Jackson made a lump clog in her throat. Both men had remained silent most of the day, speaking to each other only in short commands.

But as the trail curved around the base of a hill, a structure caught her focus. Although that word might be a generous description for the log shack tucked in a crook where two mountains met at their bases. It seemed that the only thing that kept the teetering building from blowing over was the fact that the mountain sheltered it from the wind on three sides.

Their guide reined in at the front, and Jackson did the same. The larger man grunted something she couldn't understand as he slid from his horse and strode toward her.

"You take the horses."

An extra shiver slid down her spine at Jackson's words, although it may have been the sound of his voice more than what he said. The thought of being alone in the cabin with this leech was the stuff of her nightmares.

The big man approached her and, before she could protest or even prepare for his reach, he gripped her under the arms and hauled her off the horse.

She bit back a squeal as her feet met nothing but air. Then she connected hard with the ground, and her legs gave way. The man kept a hold on her upper arm, and even though the steel in his fingers bit into her flesh through her coat, the strength of his grip kept her upright.

Jackson slid off the horse and took her other arm. His hold was much gentler, yet it left her feeling stained in a way she despised.

He led her to the door of the cabin, and she fought the urge to jerk her arm from his hand. But with her wrists bound behind her back, fighting his grip would only anger him. No, playing along had always been the best way to handle this man. Soon, though, she would catch him off guard. She would escape.

Jesus, help me escape. Please.

CHAPTER 19

"*C*an you still see her trail?"

Ezra clenched his jaw at Opal's question. It was a valid concern, and he hated the only answer he could give. So he held his tongue. Yet Opal's gaze seemed to kindle a fire on the back of his neck, even through his coat.

He scanned the ground again, then up at the mountains surrounding them. Several inches of snow covered the area, while more fell in a steady curtain. It concealed any tracks that might have been left by Tori and whomever she'd been riding with.

He had to answer, but he kept his gaze scanning the landscape. "Snow's covered the tracks. If I knew who she was with, it might help me figure out where they went." For that matter, he didn't know for sure she'd even gone this route. Maybe her tracks had been those traveling toward Mountain Bluff. If she'd ridden one of the other directions and needed him—right now—he could have made a life-threatening mistake coming up to this mountain wilderness.

God, where is she?

"Do you think she went with them willingly?" Opal's measured voice called him back from the agony swirling in his mind.

He turned to look at her. "Do you?"

She shook her head. "She doesn't trust men. Unless it was a woman in need, she wouldn't have gone willingly with anyone."

He studied Opal. Her jaw seemed clamped tight, more resolute than usual. More like Tori.

She doesn't trust men. He wanted so desperately to dig into that statement. He knew Tori had experienced things in her past that left scars she still hadn't overcome. But he didn't know exactly what. Now wasn't the time to probe. And it wasn't Opal's story to tell. At least, he didn't think so.

Regardless, he had to focus on where Tori had gone and who she might be with. He scanned the land again, his gaze catching on what looked to be a trail around the base of the mountains to their right.

"If Tori did meet a woman in need of help, is there a colony or settlement up here where she might live?"

Ezra shook his head. "No settlements. Only the occasional trapper's cabin, but sometimes those are hard to spot until you almost pass them."

She looked around the area. "I suppose we should keep going."

He nodded and strode forward, aiming toward what would hopefully be the same trail Tori had traveled a few hours before. Had it only been a few hours? Or days? Maybe he was already too late. If she'd been accosted by some lecherous criminal hiding out in the mountains, some man whose morals were completely overshadowed by the lusts of a base nature...

His stomach roiled at the images flashing through his mind, and he marched faster, almost breaking into a run as the ground sloped downward.

"Ezra, wait." Opal's words paused him midstride, but it was the tone that made his blood run cold.

"What?"

"There. Look beside that rock. What is that?" She slid off the horse and started toward the cluster of stones where she pointed.

He made it there first, his gaze homing in on the square of white cloth he'd completely missed before. He dropped to his haunches, reached for the fabric, and unfurled it with his gloved fingers.

It appeared to be a man's handkerchief, edged in green thread. Initials had been embroidered in one corner using the same color.

A gasp from behind tensed his muscles, and he swiveled to see what danger had startled Opal. Her pale blue eyes had grown large, focused intently on the handkerchief in his hands. Her face had faded as pale as the snow, and she took a tiny step back.

He rose. "What is it? Do you know who this belonged to?" He wanted to examine the initials to see if they rang familiar, but he was afraid to take his eyes off the pale woman in front of him. She looked like she might swoon any second.

"It's his." Her gaze swung from the cloth to Ezra's face, and she gripped his wrist with enough strength to still the blood flow. "We have to find her, Ezra. That's Jackson's. He must have her." She spun and charged toward the horse.

Jackson? His mind struggled to place the name, but it came up empty. Was he the man who'd taken advantage of Tori? A burning heat surged through his veins, making him lightheaded for a second as his body seemed to struggle with his reaction.

In two strides, he was by Opal's side as she mounted the mare. "Who. Is. Jackson?" The voice that came from his mouth was low, menacing. Nothing like his own.

She sank into the saddle with an expression so laced with despair, it made his knees threaten to give way. "My father called him his steward. We called him Lucifer."

Lucifer. Satan himself? His body flushed cold, then hot. "He's the one who hurt Tori."

She didn't give an actual response, but the desolation in her eyes confirmed his worst fears.

The cad. The blackguard. The lowlife, villainous, despoiler of innocence.

He forced himself to breathe, taking in slow drafts lest he actually explode from the tempest of emotions churning inside. He'd never felt such…rage. The word seemed insufficient to describe the tumult.

Turning away from Opal, he clenched his eyes shut, then squeezed the bridge of his nose between his thumb and forefinger. He had to get a handle on himself or he wouldn't do Tori any good.

With slow, deliberate movements, he lowered his hand from his face, then turned back to Opal. It was hard to meet the fear in her eyes, but he wanted to know everything. Had to read in her face what she might be afraid to say.

"Why would he have come thousands of miles to find her? What does he want?" It had to be more than the man's base lust. No matter how tempting Tori might be. The thought of any man with her made the bile churn into a funnel in his gut. He forced his mind back from that brink, focusing on Opal's response to his questions.

Uncertainty touched her expression. "I...don't know. Maybe my father sent him?"

He followed that line of thought. "Did your father not want you to leave?" Any man in his right mind wouldn't allow his daughter and niece to head off into the Wyoming Territory unchaperoned, but he needed to understand more about the man.

Her eyes widened and she shook her head, pulling back a few inches as though she needed to put space between her and the question. "He didn't know we were leaving."

There were so many gaps in the story, so many glaring questions, his mind spun as he struggled to find where to start. He forced himself to keep a steady tone. "Opal, I need you to tell me why you left, so I can understand what's happening here." *And be quick about it. Every minute matters for Tori.* He clamped his mouth shut to keep that last part from slipping out. She looked like she might bolt if he pressed too hard.

"Jackson has always paid us more attention than we wanted, but Tori..." Her words died off and she looked away. Her throat worked, and she turned back to him, red rimming her eyes. "He liked Tori best. But then she came of age and left Riverdale, and he started noticing me again. I mentioned it to her when I went to visit, and she decided we...had to leave." Opal's voice had grown stronger, but it seemed to crack on those last few words. She swallowed again, then jutted her chin forward, her blue eyes flashing like Tori's did sometimes.

"So we did. We left that night, and came to see you."

Such a powerful flood of relief surged through his chest, his eyes sank closed again as he thought of it. If they'd gone anywhere else, what might have happened to them? But it didn't bear thinking. They'd come to him, and it had to be God's leading. Now he had to get Tori away from this man once and for all. *Lord, don't let me be too late. Wrap her in Your protective hand until I get there.*

After inhaling a long, cleansing breath, he opened his eyes again. "Would your father have sent Jackson to find the two of you? Or is there any other reason the rake came all this way?"

She nibbled her lower lip. "I don't know of another reason. I'm sure Papa wasn't happy we left."

He nodded. "I wouldn't expect him to be alone. Especially not up in these mountains. There are two sets of hoofprints as far as I can tell." Although he didn't have the tracking experience his brother Zeche did. Give him a ledger and he could make sense of it in less than a minute, but not faint hoof scrapes on mountain rocks.

He turned to scan the area again, trying to see it through the eyes of a man who'd just kidnapped a woman. If he'd stumbled on Tori's campsite, he would still want to find Opal. Maybe the man wouldn't touch her if he needed information Tori could provide, although he couldn't rely on that. He had to get to her soon.

The weight of responsibility sank heavier on his shoulders, but he forced the thought away. *Focus, Reid.*

This Jackson must be with someone who knew this area. Maybe someone who knew of a cabin up in these mountains. A place they would keep Tori until they'd accomplished the rest of their mission. Especially if they were trying to get details from Tori about Opal's location.

She'd never tell. He knew with a certainty that went all the way to his core. She'd endure any form of torture—even death—before she gave up her cousin to that man's vile ways.

A burn crept up the back of his throat. It was that stubborn determination—that devoted, unquenchable love—that made her so special. And now the same spirit put her in such danger.

If Jackson were the monster he suspected, the man wouldn't be satisfied with a little misconduct. Now that Tori had slipped from his lair and taken his latest victim with her, the man would demand retribution.

The icy thought drove him forward.

~

Tori forced her back to hold its stiffness as Jackson approached, even though her stomach churned so much she wanted to vomit. If the bile actually did rise up her throat, maybe she'd cast up her accounts on *him*.

He stopped close enough that only a few inches parted them, despite the fact that she had pressed her back against the rough log mantle over the hearth. The young flames of the fire leapt inside, but she could barely feel the heat through the chill in her body. He'd untied her hands, and she gripped the folds of her skirt to keep them still.

"I'm losing my patience, Tori. As much as I'd prefer to give you time to settle in to this…quaint little cottage, I need to know where your cousin is. She might be in danger, so I must find her quickly."

She didn't flatter the comment with a reaction. Just kept her focus on the bulk of the other man at the far end of the single-room shack. She'd never seen him before they accosted her in the woods, but now she had the outline of his brawny shoulders seared into her mind. He sat facing the small table, his back to them, hunched over something in his hands.

It looked almost like he was whittling something. But what? Surely they would want to eat soon. Would they expect her to cook for them? Maybe she could find something with which to poison the food. The thought almost brought a smile to her lips, but she forced her face to remain void.

"Tori." Jackson's tone held steel under that fake suave he liked to flaunt. "Perhaps it would be better if I send the grizzly outside so we can have private time together."

It took every ounce of her strength not to react. Not to find that distant hiding place as his hand touched her shoulder, sliding over so his thumb brushed her neck, then down her bodice. His hands were always warm, almost clammy. Disgusting.

She bit hard on her tongue, not even willing to give him the satisfaction of seeing her bite her lip. The tang of blood filled her senses, giving her something else to think about besides Jackson's hand as it traveled slowly southward.

What was Ezra doing now? He should have made it to the Rocky Ridge days before. How long would he stay before gathering Opal and traveling back to Mountain Bluff.

If only she'd never left the place. She might have seen Ezra anytime now. He had been planning to come back to her. Planning to bring Opal. She could have waited.

But this vile impetuous tendency she'd been cursed with had made her chase after him. If she'd been born a different person, perhaps her life would have taken different turns.

Maybe her parents wouldn't have chosen their profitable schemes instead of her. Maybe her uncle would have been kinder. Maybe this Lucifer would never have looked twice at her. If only she'd been born a boy.

Do you know God loves you, Tori? She almost snorted at the words that flashed through her mind again. Ezra's words. But if God's love was anything close to the lust glimmering from the eyes of the beast in front of her, He could keep it far away. She was much better off without an Almighty God.

He wants to be there when you need him. Even more than that, He wants you to be happy.

The words pierced even deeper than they had when he'd spoken them, cracking the icy cage she'd constructed around her emotions. Happy? How dare he think she could be happy. Happiness had teased her in those moments she thought maybe Ezra would forgive her. Would agree to marry her after everything.

But that would never happen now. She'd been hauled off to the middle of a mountain wilderness, bound and practically helpless, by Satan himself, who now had the power to do anything he pleased with her.

Was this God's way of making her happy? If the Almighty appeared before her, she might spit in his face.

An anguish deeper than anything she'd ever felt wrenched her chest, building into a sob that she contained by clamping her jaw in a vise-like hold.

"Come now, kitten. It's not as bad as all that. If you prefer we talk about where your cousin is, just say the word."

She turned her cold, hard fury on him, lashing out with her heel in an attempt to kick him in a sensitive area. But her boot caught in her skirts, and all she managed to land was a muffled blow on his shin.

Like a bear angered by a slingshot, he drew back long enough for his rage to build. Then he charged.

His hands gripped her neck, and the rough bark of the mantle dug into her shoulders. She tried to duck low, to slip out of his hold, but his fingers dug deeper into the soft concave just under her jaw, wrapping her spine and cutting off all air.

Her throat spasmed, and true fear flooded her veins. Nay, terror. Unlike anything she'd felt since the first time he'd accosted her so many years ago.

He was going to kill her. After all the times she'd wanted to die, yet pulled herself back from the edge. Forced herself to move forward, for Opal's sake, if not for her own. This time, he'd do it. This time, when she'd finally caught a glimpse of what might have been the chance for a better life, maybe even the happiness Ezra said God wanted for her.

God, I don't want to die. If you're as real as Ezra says, help me. Please.

She fought back with every part of her body, kicking and grabbing at his hands, at anything she could reach. But his longer arms gave him the advantage, even though the lack of breath gave her a desperation that should have overcome anything.

Minutes passed, or maybe hours. Flashes of black pulsed through her vision. *God, help me. I need you now.*

Her body screamed for air as her mind shouted the anthem. *Take me, Lord. Do with me as You will. I have nothing left.*

And then the blackness closed in around her.

CHAPTER 20

*T*he sound of male voices arguing drifted from the shack as Ezra peered around the snowcapped rock. He strained to make out any words, but the tones were too muffled.

The door flew open, and a huge man lumbered out, stomping through the snow as he followed a set of faint tracks around the side of the building. He didn't fit the description Opal had given of Jackson, so he must be an accomplice. He needed to know for sure, though.

Pulling away from the rock, he slipped back around the base of the mountain to where Opal sat atop the mare.

He grabbed the reins and motioned for her to climb down as he whispered, "Come tell me if you recognize this man."

She nodded and then slid down from the horse, her movements quiet except a soft crunch of snow when she landed.

He led her to the edge of the rock and peered around it. The man would likely come back around the cabin and go inside any moment. Unless he'd been sent on an errand, then he would come riding out on a horse.

What if he came their direction? Ezra should have thought of that already. He reached for the Colt Army in his waistband and cocked it.

If he waited 'til the man was close enough, the bullet would do the damage it needed. Although, his gut tightened at the thought of wreaking that kind of injury on a human being. But if these men had hurt Tori, he would do anything necessary to get her away from them —and keep Opal safe in the process.

In another minute, the man stomped from behind the shack, and Ezra scooted back to give Opal room to look. "Do you recognize him?"

She was quiet for several ticks of his pulse, then the sound of the door bumping shut drifted over the snow to them. Opal straightened. "It was hard to get a good look with all that hair on his face, but I don't think I know him. Certainly not from Boiling Springs."

He must be a local then. And this was probably his mountain hide-away. If he was a criminal seeking refuge from the law, the man might have few qualms about doing Jackson's dirty work.

Ezra peered around the edge of the boulder again. He needed to get closer to the cabin. As far as he could see, the place didn't have any windows to peek through, although it didn't look like the logs were chinked very well, so he might find an opening wide enough to see through.

But how to get there? The expanse of snow lay before them, unbroken except for the tracks the men must have made when they'd arrived, and those had a thin layer of snow already filling them. The snowfall had slowed to steady flurries, but maybe if he stayed in the first set of tracks, the snow would cover over his new prints. And the low cloud cover made the day dreary enough it might be harder to see the tracks from a distance.

How many men were inside? He'd heard two distinct male voices, but there could be other men, quieter men.

He turned back to Opal. "I'm going to get closer so I can see what we're up against. Stay here. Don't follow me for any reason."

She nodded, and for once he was thankful she didn't possess the full streak of stubborn tenacity—or rather, bullheadedness—of her cousin.

"If shots break out, get back on the horse and high-tail it out of here. Don't wait for me. I'll be behind you as soon as I can. Got it?"

Her acquiescence came slower this time, and her eyes didn't meet his as she gave only a single nod.

"I mean it, Opal. If anything happens to you, I'll have your cousin's wrath to face, and that's not something I relish." Although at this moment, he would gladly subject himself to her ire. He'd subject himself to anything, if only Tori were with them, whole and unscarred, both physically and emotionally. He had to keep a confident front for Opal's sake.

"I'll ride to a safe place if I hear shots."

That was probably the best agreement he was going to get, so he nodded, then turned and eyed the faint prints leading to the front of the cabin.

He gathered his muscles to sprint forward.

"Wait."

Opal's voice caught him up short, and he spun to face her. Had she seen something else?

"Should we pray first?" The innocence in the question caught him off guard, then sent a wash of remorse through him.

He'd been about to charge, putting not only himself at risk, but heightening the danger for Tori. All without a single nod to the Almighty, the God Who even now held her in His hand.

He blew out a breath and nodded, dipping his head as he squeezed his eyes tight. "Father, forgive me for attempting to step out ahead of You. Keep Tori safe in the protection of Your hands. Guide us in Your wisdom so we can help her. Bring her back to us safely, Lord. Please."

As he remained in the spirit of prayer, letting God's peace settle over him, a quiet strength seemed to infuse his muscles, shoring up his mind so the desperation of moments before evaporated. *Father, go Thou with me. Guide my actions.*

Inhaling a deep breath, he raised his gaze and met Opal's watery blue eyes. She offered him a wobbly smile, and he nodded in return. "I'm off then. Keep an eye out."

With a prayer on his lips and his pistol drawn, he stayed low as he darted forward. All seemed quiet outside the cabin, and he reached the corner of the building, then crouched low around the side.

He could hear male voices within. They sounded agitated, although no longer raised in argument. He strained to pick-up Tori's strong alto, but if she was in there, she was silent. Shifting along the cabin wall, he found a gap the thickness of his little finger between the logs. He pressed his eye against the opening. It was hard to see more than shifting blurs inside. But some of the words filtered to him.

"...don't know why ya had to go an' knock her cold. Is she still breathin'?"

Cold terror clutched Ezra's chest, and he craned closer to hear the response.

"Of course. Get over here with that whiskey. She needs something to rouse her senses."

What had they done to her? He tried again to peer through the hole and barely made out a figure shifting inside. But the men seemed to be at the far end, and with the interior so dim, he couldn't make out details.

He had to get Tori out of there, but to do that, he needed a better feel for what he was up against. Were there just two men?

After sidling along the cabin wall toward the back, he peered around the rear corner. Two horses huddled against the cold inside a split rail corral. He didn't see any other signs of life, save a small brown bird hopping in the hoof prints in the pen, probably searching for a morsel to eat.

Down the back wall he crept, the sounds inside growing louder. Yet the logs fit together almost flush in this area, leaving him no openings to look through. So he moved on around to the far side. This wall held a rock chimney, uneven and roughly masoned. Near the front corner of the cabin, the voices grew louder inside. They must be standing near him, only the thick logs separating him from them. He pressed a gloved hand to one of the trunks, feeling the rough bark through the leather.

"Pour a little more in the side of her mouth. She should wake up soon." The smooth male voice seemed to reek of culture.

"Ya better hope ya didn't do her in. We might never find the other one if she's not around to lead us there." This deeper, rougher tone probably belonged to the burly man who'd left the cabin a few minutes before.

"I only decommissioned her struggling for a few moments. She'll be fine when she returns to her senses."

A grunt was his only reply. Probably the other man didn't know what decommissioning a woman's struggling meant exactly. It was a question Ezra dreaded the answer to.

Shuffling noises sounded inside, and Ezra peered around the corner. All seemed quiet in front. How could he draw the men out of the cabin? He'd be shot down in seconds if he tried to charge in without knowing the layout. And it didn't seem there was a way to sneak in without the men seeing him—not with the only entrance through the front door.

He glanced around the clearing. Behind him a small stand of trees stood laden with snow. In the rear of the cabin, the corral holding the horses backed up to the rock wall of a mountain.

Perhaps if he made a noise, it might draw the men out. But what was he going to do then? Shoot them? As angry as their actions made him, bringing death on a man settled in his gut with a queasy feeling. Maybe he could wing them enough to disable until he got them secured for the sheriff.

One of the horses in back gave a soft nicker, and the responding whinny that rang across the clearing made his blood run cold.

Opal's horse. He'd not thought to keep the animal farther back lest it give them away. One more thing he'd failed at with this sneak attack.

The cabin door cracked open and a deep voice called from inside, "Who's there?"

Ezra ducked back behind the corner, then held himself as still as he could, barely daring to breathe.

Long moments pulsed by, then the voice again. "Show yerself."

A murmured tone sounded from inside, but Ezra couldn't catch the words.

"If I go out there, they might shoot me down." The deep tone was easier to decipher.

"…must…check…paying you…" The weasely tone had to belong to Jackson, and it elicited another grumble from his cohort.

Then a rustling noise came from the front of the cabin, and Ezra peered around the corner, exposing as little of himself as possible.

The burly man they'd seen before, clad in thick layers of buckskins, stepped through the snow. His stride seemed purposeful, and Ezra tensed as he realized where the man was headed—straight for Opal's hiding spot.

Lord, let her have moved. If she'd obeyed his instructions, she would have retreated around the side of the hill. But that meant she wouldn't be able to see the man stalking toward her. And unless she were mounted and already riding away, there was no doubt this bear of a man would overpower her with his rifle.

If Opal were captured too, how in the world would he get them both away? *Lord, help me here. Protect them.*

Another whinny filled the clearing, coming from exactly where he'd left woman and horse.

She hadn't moved. And the bear-man now broke into a run. A lumbering charge that covered ground with surprising speed.

He had no choice. Ezra raised his pistol with both hands, sighted for the shoulder of the man's gun hand, and squeezed the trigger.

The explosion rang with triple its usual force, reverberating off the snow as the sound filled the clearing.

His target sank to his knees, clutching his side. He didn't scream or cry out, but the massive body crumpled to the snow.

Had he wounded him mortally? The staccato racing in Ezra's chest pulsed through his ears like a smithy's hammer. He'd killed the man. But at least Opal was safe.

He watched the bulk for several more moments, scanning for any sign of movement. Nothing.

But a rustling inside the cabin snagged his focus. The door cracked again, but with it opening away from him, he couldn't get a look at the man who must be peering out.

Ezra inhaled a steadying breath, then called out, "We have you surrounded, Jackson. Come out with your hands up, and it'll go easier for you." Maybe he would believe the bluff.

A shot exploded from inside the cabin, splintering the wood a mere foot from Ezra's head. He bit down a cry and jumped back, then dropped to his knees.

The man was mad. And obviously not going to blindly swallow the posse story. All he'd accomplished by speaking had been to give his position away.

Staying low, he moved down the cabin wall so he was behind the stone chimney. But this was still close enough to his original position, if Jackson got trigger happy, things might get dangerous. Better to move around to the other side to keep him guessing. And give weight to the story that the man was surrounded.

The horses in back only glanced at him as he crept by. *Thank you, Lord, for keeping them silent.*

Once settled in his new position, he found the narrow slit between logs he'd noticed before and peered in. Shadows shifted inside, matching with the sounds of boot scuffs drifting from the interior. Jackson seemed to be pacing.

Where was Tori? Still unconscious? If she really was incoherent, it didn't bode well that she hadn't regained her senses after all this time. But maybe she was only pretending to be so.

God, please...please let Tori be alive. Keep her safe. Lifting his fears in prayer eased them a little. God was in control of this situation, no matter how desperate it seemed.

The pacing inside continued, and every so often Jackson would stride to the door and peer through the crack, then mutter to himself and return to pacing.

For five minutes at least, the man kept the same pattern. Yet his agitation seemed to grow so strong it was almost palpable. What would he do when desperation took over?

Ezra didn't have to wonder long, because Jackson paused his pacing mid-stride. Had he heard something? Or was he making a decision?

The man stalked to the door and pushed it so a sliver of light fell into the cabin. "I have a gun on the girl. Come into the clearing where I can see you—all of you—or I'll shoot her."

Fear tried to claw up Ezra's chest, but he pressed it down. Jackson had no way of knowing whether the posse story was real, so he must be doing his best to regain control of the situation. Men like him couldn't stand to be at a disadvantage.

Ezra held his tongue but lifted a prayer from his heart to heaven. *What do I do, Lord? Wait him out?*

"Come out in the open or I'll kill her. You have one minute." Jackson's tone had grown hard as steel, deeper than the whine from before. He moved away from the door and strode with purposeful steps to the far end of the room where Tori must be.

The fear in Ezra's veins ratcheted to terror as the man hauled up a second figure. The image wasn't much more than shadows, but he knew without a doubt it was Tori. His heart ached in a way he'd never thought possible, and it took all his strength not to leap to his feet and surge into the cabin.

CHAPTER 21

*E*ven through the crack in the logs, Ezra could see the outline of the pistol Jackson held as he moved into the stream of light from the doorway.

"I have her here at the door with a gun at her head. You have ten seconds left to show yourself, or the chit dies."

Panic clawed in Ezra. He had to do something. Now. *Father above, give me wisdom.* He inhaled a stilling breath. "If you kill her, you won't have a prayer of finding Opal. I'll make a deal with you, though." If he could just get the man outside.

"I don't want a deal. Come out or I'll toss her bullet-ridden body out for you to collect."

The light inside the cabin grew stronger, and through the slit between the logs, Jackson's outline merged with the limp form of Tori. Her head lolled sideways, which meant she hadn't yet regained consciousness.

His body craved to peer around the corner to get a better look at what the man was doing, but he was facing the opening from this direction, and surely Jackson would see him. Although maybe it would make the man waste a few shots.

Ezra left his position near the peephole and edged toward the corner of the building.

But a motion in the distance caught his attention. A horse and rider.

Opal.

She rode low over the mare's neck, her navy gown billowing behind her as the animal cantered through the clearing. What was she thinking?

Ezra peered around the corner to see Jackson raising his gun.

The man stepped to the edge of the doorway and opened it wider to watch the startling display in the yard. Then his hand snaked out, aiming a long-barreled pistol directly at Opal.

Ezra's mind exploded, pushing his body into action. He aimed his Colt at the rapscallion, squeezed the trigger.

The explosion came, and Jackson's arm jerked in the same instant. But the noise didn't stop.

A volley of shots continued, jerking Ezra's gun hand with the recoil. His gun kept shooting of its own accord, and he aimed it upward and struggled to keep the pistol from writhing in his grip. The powder from his shot must have ignited the chamber beside it, setting off a chain of gunfire. Of all the times for that to happen...

After five shots, the gun finally silenced, bringing a deep hush to the clearing. Even Opal had reined in her horse in the far corner, and sat watching. Ezra held the piece in both hands, cradling it as his mind spun through what to do next. All six of his shots were empty now. Had he even struck Jackson? He reached for the pouch at his waste to reload.

"I wouldn't do that. You're mine now, you and both the chits." The throaty growl came from mere feet away, stilling Ezra's racing pulse along with his hands. He eased his gaze up to the man.

Jackson stood in the snow, not five feet away, pistol aimed directly at Ezra's head. At this close range, there was no way the man would miss. And the glimmer in his dark gaze shone with hatred and a barely-dampened fury.

This was the end. The day he would pass from this life to eternity. But what would happen to Tori? And Opal? He couldn't leave them at the hands of this monster. Not without help.

God, have mercy on them. Bring them through this unscathed. I leave them in your hands.

The barrel of Jackson's gun wobbled, and the man shifted his grip. Did he shake from fear or anger? His knuckles were a stark white against the polished walnut stock, the pale skin decorated by a thin layer of brown hairs. What in this man's life had made him into the twisted, despicable cad standing here now, about to take the life of another?

Interesting how philosophical Ezra grew now that he stared death in the face.

He shifted under the weight of the man's stare. "If you're going to kill me, Jackson, go ahead and do it. I've no qualms about going to meet my Maker, and I know He'll spare these women from your hand. No sense in dragging this out, though."

The strong certainty that filled him was more than anything he could have conjured on his own. This peace had to come from God, including the certainty that Tori and Opal would be fine. Yet he couldn't top the ache in his chest at the thought that he'd not have another chance to speak to Tori. To tell her of the love that had grown so surely inside him. To ask her again to be his bride. Beg her, if necessary. His chance had been lost.

Jackson's grip tightened even more on the gun, and his finger shifted on the trigger.

A blast rent the air, and Ezra closed his eyes as he waited for the pain. *Into Your hands, Lord.*

Yet the blow never came. No bullet slammed into him, knocking him off his feet from the power of such a close range. Nothing.

The sound of a man's groan made him open his eyes. Jackson had crumpled to his knees, writhing into a twist as he stared up at Ezra. His eyes had widened into huge glassy orbs.

A dark crimson mark stained the man's chest, widening with each second as Ezra struggled to make sense of what had happened.

A noise came from his left, and he whirled to face the new threat.

The great, burly bear-man struggled to his feet, at least twenty feet out from the cabin, cradling his right side. Ezra leapt forward and snatched Jackson's gun. He turned it on the other man. His gaze swept to where Opal still sat atop the horse at the far end of the clearing. She wasn't exactly safe, but if she didn't move, hopefully she wouldn't snag the stranger's attention.

As the man straightened, he seemed to be trying to catch his breath. Yet he moved readily enough. Had he been faking death, lying in the snow all this time? And who had shot Jackson? Opal didn't have a gun, and the four of them were the only people here. Except Tori.

He took his eyes from the giant long enough to sweep his gaze to the cabin's doorway. Tori still lay there, in a crumpled heap. A sight that caught his breath and wouldn't give it back. Was she dead? Why hadn't she awakened after all this time and commotion?

God, didn't You say You would save her? His heart cried out the prayer as he clawed at any bit of the certainty he'd felt strongly only moments before.

Trust Me. Whether the feeling was actually sent from the Almighty or not, trust was all he could do right now. He had to deal with the giant who lumbered toward him, only a dozen feet away.

He sharpened his focus on the man, sighting down the trigger of the handgun.

"I'm not gonna hurt ya. Nor the women." The man stopped, breathing hard as though he'd climbed halfway up a mountain. He nodded toward Jackson's crumpled body. "Never did like him from the first, but he was offerin' a small fortune that was hard to pass up. Feels kinda good ta put him outta his misery."

So the bear-man had shot Jackson? Ezra took the man's measure again. He'd just saved Ezra's life. Did that make him trustworthy? Considering he'd obviously had a hand in kidnapping Tori, and maybe even in sending her into this unconscious state, Ezra wasn't inclined to trust him.

Ezra kept the gun pointed at the man. "Stay where you are." He shifted sideways, flicking his gaze to Jackson to make sure the man didn't move as he neared. He wouldn't make the same mistake twice. Before he assumed Jackson dead, he'd feel for himself whether any lifeblood still pumped through his veins.

But there was no pulse at Jackson's neck, and his body already seemed to be growing cold.

Ezra straightened, returning his full focus on the other fellow.

The man extended his hands. "You can tie me up if it makes ya feel better. We need ta get the girlie there fixed up, though." He nodded toward Tori. "Jackson choked her in a fit o' rage, but she was still breathin' strong last I checked."

Every muscle in Ezra's body tensed as he wavered between securing this man or rushing to Tori's side.

"There's a good solid rope around back. Go ahead an' tie me ta one of those trees yonder so you can focus on her."

That settled it then. He motioned Opal over, and she held the man at gunpoint while he secured the huge paws to a stout tree.

"How bad's the wound?" Ezra eyed the blood seeping through the man's buckskin tunic. Maybe he needed a cloth to staunch the flow.

"Bullet didn't hit anythin' important. Go on and tend yer lady."

Ezra tested the tie a final time, then rose and turned toward the cabin. He took the pistol from Opal. "Let's help Tori."

She ran behind him, but he didn't stay and wait for her. Every minute—every second—could make the difference for Tori.

She still lay crumpled on the cabin floor as if she'd been dropped there. Which she probably had.

He sank to his knees and straightened her body, easing her over so he could see her face. "Tori, love."

The rise and fall of her chest was faint, but the tiny movement spread such relief through his veins, he almost lost his balance. He stroked her cheek, flushed red from the cold. "Wake up, Tori."

"I'll get some snow to bring her around." Opal disappeared outside again, then returned with a skirt full of fluffy, white ice.

He scooped some with his hand and wiped it across Tori's brow. "Why would she still be unconscious? Do you think they drugged her?"

"I don't know." She knelt on Tori's other side, then cupped snow in her hand and pulled Tori's collar down. "This should do the—" A gasp cut off the last word.

Ezra leaned close to see what had caused Opal's reaction. The dark blue marks on Tori's neck made Ezra's blood run cold. "She's been choked." He spat the words, trying to keep his anger tamped down. He'd heard the men talking about it, but seeing glaring evidence was enough to set fire in his veins.

His gaze wandered across the marks on her pale skin, especially right in the middle where her windpipe must be. He couldn't help but shoot a glare toward the man lying facedown in the snow outside. What a sorry excuse for a life.

Why, Lord? Why would God create someone who did such vile and despicable things? Why would a good Father ever craft such a person?

He stared at the lifeless form. The man's pale hands and face. The way his eyelids closed in something of a tortured look. Like he was as miserable now as he'd made others during his life. But maybe... perhaps he'd been just as tormented during his life. Maybe inner demons, or something horrible in his past, had driven him to make the decisions that had damaged Tori and Opal.

Lord willing, Tori would rise above the pain this man had caused, not just the physical wounds but the emotional wounds harder to see. But Jackson...he'd never have the chance to repent. Even now, the torment on his face was likely that of his spirit in the lake of fire.

But for the grace of God go I.

"I think she's stirring."

Ezra pulled his gaze from the fallen corpse back to Tori, who was turning her head the slightest bit. Her face and neck were sprinkled with snow and water, and gooseflesh raised on the skin just visible below her neck.

She moved again, and he reached for her hand. "Can you hear me, Tori? Wake up."

Those beautiful, walnut-colored lashes fluttered, opening to reveal eyes that warmed him like nothing ever had.

"Tori." He leaned closer, stroking her hand with his thumb as he fought back the emotion clogging his throat.

Her expression seemed bewildered as her gaze roamed from him to Opal, then back to him. She opened her mouth to speak, but the only sound was a wheezing rasp. She cleared her throat, a flicker of pain crossing her face with the action.

"What's wrong?" He tensed, all his muscles coiling for action.

She opened her mouth again. "Where...are we?" Her voice was barely understandable through the rasp, and she pressed a hand to her throat.

"Don't talk, Tori. Just rest. You were kidnapped, but you're safe now. Jackson choked you, but he's dead. You're safe." He stroked the hair from her cheek, craving to reach even closer. To feel for himself that she really was alive.

God, thank you, she's alive.

Tori stared up at him, eyes wide and unblinking, yet her expression was inscrutable. He didn't see fear in her gaze, nor wonder. Not even anger.

At last, she opened her mouth as she seemed to pull all her effort to speak. "He's dead?"

The import of that single fact in Tori's life struck him with a powerful blow.

"He's dead, Tori. You're safe. God protected you. He brought you back to me." He couldn't stand it any longer. He leaned down to press a kiss to her forehead.

When he raised up to look at her again, silent tears streamed from the corners of her eyes. The sight fractured something in his chest, and he pulled her into his arms, cradling her head against his chest.

She clutched his shirt with both her hands, clinging to him as her shoulders began to shake. The well seemed endless as she sobbed, releasing emotions that had likely been building for years. He could feel the torment with each fresh wave, the changing tide of grief and fear and the overwhelming rush of relief.

He held her close, rocking and pressing kisses into her hair. His chest had clogged so thickly, he couldn't have spoken if he wanted to. It was enough to hold her. To be here for her. Be here with her.

And whether she agreed to it or not, he wasn't planning to let anything separate them again.

CHAPTER 22

*T*he ride back through the mountains was a quiet affair, yet Ezra couldn't have been more content. After eating some of the meal Opal pieced together, Tori seemed to regain some of her strength. Yet even now, cradled in front of him in the saddle, secure in his arms, she seemed so fragile. It might take a while for her to recover from all the trauma she'd been through, but the tears had been a start. And he planned to be there every step of the way, praying for her and offering the support of a friend. And more, when she was ready.

For now, he could be satisfied with how far they'd come in only a few short hours.

Jackson's accomplice, the brawny man who said his name was Hanks, was tied onto a horse and tethered behind Ezra's mount. His bullet wound turned out to be a clean shot through the flesh, something Ezra had been able to patch himself. It would do until they reached a doctor.

The man had seemed contrite about his part in Tori's capture and subsequent abuse. He said Jackson had hired him to help find Opal because he knew the area. The man had paid him substantially to keep silent and do the heavy work, but Hanks hadn't liked the way Jackson treated Tori, especially when he'd flown hot and begun choking her. And since Hanks had eventually shot Jackson and saved them all, Ezra was inclined to withhold his judgment and let the sheriff mete out justice. That would ultimately be God's role anyway. They'd left Jackson's body at the cabin for the sheriff to retrieve later, after they shared the sordid tale.

Ezra glanced to the rear of their line at Opal. She returned a soft smile, reassuring him with her steady presence. She'd been such a good friend to Tori through it all, and to him as well. He couldn't help a tender spot in his heart for the woman.

Tori stirred in his arms, and he leaned around to see her face. "Would you like to stop for a break?"

She looked up at him, her heart-shaped face so close. So tempting. It took everything in him not to lean down and kiss those sassy lips. But there would be time for that later.

"I don't need to stop." She paused, still looking at him. Studying him. "What happens now?"

"I'd like to get to South Pass tonight, although it'll be late. We can turn over Hanks to the sheriff, then you and Opal can get some much-needed rest."

"You, too."

A grin touched the corner of his mouth. "I won't turn down sleep when it's time."

Her lips softened in the hint of a smile, too, but the look didn't reach her eyes. "What then?"

He studied her, flicking his gaze up a couple times to make sure they stayed on the trail. But he needed to know where she was going with her questions. "What do you want to happen?" Was she eager to get to her new life in Mountain Bluff? He still hadn't asked why she left it in the first place.

She turned away from him, looking ahead so he could no longer see her expression. "I want to go back to the Rocky Ridge." Her words came so softly, he wasn't sure he heard correctly.

"To rest?"

"To stay."

His heart skipped a beat, and he pulled his horse to a stop, not caring a whit about the two horses that bumped into them from behind.

Tori twisted in the saddle to face him, and he rested a hand on each of her shoulders.

He searched her gaze, praying he'd see the truth there. "You don't want to leave again?"

Her gaze softened, and she shook her head the slightest bit. "I don't."

He inhaled a deep breath through his nose. *Praise be.* He wasn't waiting another moment to ask her, but he had to gather his wits.

He ran one hand down her arm, found her hand, and clasped it. "Tori, the last time I asked you to marry me, there was one important thing I left out. I didn't tell you just exactly how much I've come to love you. I'm not sure I knew it then, but I know it with everything in me now. So I'm going to ask you again. Will you *please* marry me?"

One side of her mouth tipped up, and her eyes glittered under layers of moisture. The hint of a smile had to be a good sign, right? That was more than she'd given him last time.

She squeezed his hand. "Since you said please, I suppose I'll agree." The little minx offered a sassy smile, and he took in every inch of it.

Joy exploded in his chest, bubbling into his throat as he raised his hand from her shoulder to cradle her cheek.

She leaned into his touch, but the smile slipped from her face as it took on a pained sadness. "It's not... I'm not..." She paused, her throat working before she tried again. "It's not going to be easy...for me." She dropped her gaze from his, looking somewhere around his chin. "I mean... There are some things you need to know...about me. Maybe we should wait and talk about it later. You may change your mind."

His chest ached at the pain on her face. Everything she'd endured for so long. He pulled her close to him, holding her tight against his chest. "Shh... I know what you've gone through, Tori. But this is a new start. It's behind us, and we'll work through whatever we need to together."

She rested still against him for several moments, then shifted as she looked up at him. "Are you sure?" She studied his eyes, her own gaze so uncertain.

"Positive."

Despite the sadness still hovering there, her expression was laced with enough hope to spring the same emotion in his chest.

His eyes roamed her face again, slowing on her perfect mouth. Did he dare kiss her? It wasn't Opal or Hanks looking on that held him back. She'd been handled so vilely in the past, he didn't want his touch to resurrect any of those emotions.

Tori reached up to press a cold hand to his cheek, and he met her gaze. Did she know what he'd been thinking? How did she feel about it? Maybe he should come right out and ask. If they were going to work through her past, they needed to start talking about it anyway.

"Tori, can—?"

"Yes."

He paused, checking her gaze to make sure she knew what she was agreeing to.

"Yes." She spoke softer this time, more tentative. But her look was full of determination. His spunky lady.

Taking his time, he lowered his mouth, tasting the warmth of her breath before the softness of her lips. And the sensation sent heat all through him. She was exquisite, every taste and smell and feel of her. He kept the kiss gentle, marveling at the fact that Tori was finally in his arms. God had been so good.

EPILOGUE

*E*zra piled the last log in his arms and stepped out of the lean-to attached to the side of Mara's house. With evening nearing, the temperatures seemed to be plummeting. It'd been two days since they finished cleaning up business with the sheriff in South Pass City and finally made it home. The weather had been nice since then, but hopefully, they weren't in for another snow.

Tori and Opal both seemed mostly recovered from the ordeal, although it still knotted his insides every time his gaze caught on the bruises marring the delicate skin at Tori's neck. Even though she seemed like a weight had slipped from her shoulders, he still had a feeling the marks on her skin would heal long before the bruises on her heart.

But he planned to do everything he could to encourage the process.

"I'll grab an armful, then that should be enough to see us through the night."

Ezra turned to see his brother-in-law striding around the front corner of the house. He nodded at the man. "Dinner about ready in there?"

Josiah bobbed his chin. "Mara sent me to retrieve you."

Ezra started toward the front of the cabin, but stalled when a noise sounded behind him. In the distance, from the woods behind the house. He turned back in time to see three riders emerge from the dim forest wall.

His muscles stiffened as he prepared to drop the wood and reach for the Colt tucked in his waistband. Visitors usually came in from the river at the front of the house, especially if they were traveling the Oregon trail.

But his gaze landed on the front rider, sitting atop a familiar bay. The hood of the man's animal-skin coat was tucked around his face, but even so, it was impossible not to recognize those broad shoulders.

Ezra tossed his firewood to the ground and moved toward them, lengthening his stride to almost a run as his heart pounded in his chest. "Zeche."

They met in the center of the clearing, and Zeche slid from his horse, his teeth flashing as a grin split his tanned face. Ezra clasped his brother in a two-armed hug, brief though it was, then stepped back to get a good look at him.

"You're alive. I wasn't quite sure you'd make it back." Emotion clogged his throat, but he swallowed it down as he cataloged the changes in Zeche's features. His sun-darkened skin hadn't paled from the winter months. If anything, his cheeks held a ruddy burn, probably from the intensity of the sun shimmering off the snow.

Zeche gripped his shoulder. "You're looking good, little brother. Being on your own must agree with you."

Ezra met his gaze. "You have no idea." Then he looked past his brother at the two riders still sitting atop their horses. A woman and a tall man, maybe old enough to be her father. "Who're your friends?"

Zeche moved around his horse to the woman's side and lifted her down with a hand on each side of her waist. There was something about the way he handled the little lady that seemed proprietary, or at least like he knew her awfully well. The older man also dismounted, but hung back beside his horse as he looked over at the woman.

So many questions swirled in Ezra's mind, but he held his tongue as Josiah stepped up beside him.

Zeche moved forward, too, his arm wrapped around the woman's back. "Fellows, I'd like you to meet Gretta Michelly and her father, Antonio Michelly." He motioned toward the older man, who approached to join their little group. "We stopped in to see everyone, then we're headed on to South Pass…" His gaze slid to meet the lady's and they gave each other sappy smiles. "…where Gretta's agreed to marry me."

Ezra couldn't bite back a chuckle, and he reached out to shake the woman's hand, then that of her father. "I suppose I should say welcome to the family."

When Josiah stepped in behind him to offer the same greeting, Ezra shifted to stand beside his brother, offering a punch to his arm. "You know Mara's gonna have a hissy when she finds out you've asked the woman to marry you before she gave her approval."

Zeche's grin went sideways. "She'll get over it."

Josiah turned to them both. "Speaking of Mara, Zeche, you and the Michellys go on inside. We'll take care of your mounts. If you keep Mara waiting, I'll not hear the end of it."

～

*T*ori leaned into the crook of Ezra's arm as they all settled around the hearth fire later that night. The cabin's main room was full with the family all together.

Family.

It was still hard to fathom the love and acceptance that came so easy with these people. But cradled here in Ezra's protective arm, everything seemed so real. So wonderful.

"Did I tell you Tori's learned how to operate the telegraph, too?" Mara announced to the group from her position on the floor by Josiah's feet. Her daughter sat in front of her, picking at the rug while Mara braided the girl's hair for the night. "She's a natural, better than me already."

Tori dipped her gaze, not quite ready to have everyone staring at her. "Not at all."

The tips of Ezra's fingers stroked her upper arm in a way that sent goose flesh skittering along her skin. "She has talent for sure, and I'll be happy for someone to share the job."

She sent him a sideways glance, the warmth of his words soaking through her chest in a way that soothed all the raw places. That same warmth cloaked his gaze, pulling a smile from her, but she pulled her focus back down. Now wasn't the time to get lost in his eyes when his whole family watched them.

Shyness wasn't her usual mien, but it seemed she couldn't quite find her equilibrium among these people. It mattered so much that they not think ill of her.

"Well..." Zeche pushed to his feet. "I'm going to head out and make sure the horses are settled." He glanced down at his bride-to-be. "Would you like to see the barn, Gretta? Maybe we'll get some ideas for what we want in the one we build."

She sent him a sweet smile and took his hand as she rose.

"You'll get some ideas, all right," Josiah mumbled under his breath, but it was loud enough for the entire room to hear.

Tori didn't miss the look Mara sent him over her shoulder.

He tapped her cheek with a wink. "Maybe we should go look at the barn, too."

This time Mara reached back and elbowed his leg.

Ezra's warm chuckle reverberated through his chest, filtering through Tori's back where she rested against him. A longing so intense pulled at her. This was where she belonged. With this man. And if she had the chance to be part of his family, too, this truly would be the happiness he said God wanted for her.

I believe you now, God. It was so humbling to see the possibility of it, and the gratefulness pulsing through her chest might just overwhelm her.

"I'd better finish in the kitchen." Opal rose quietly from her ladder-back chair and left the circle of light.

As much as she loved the feeling of sitting here tucked into Ezra's side, something about Opal's demeanor tugged at Tori. Her cousin was usually quiet, but now her tone seemed even more reticent than usual.

Tori gave Ezra an apologetic smile as she straightened. "I should go help her."

He searched her gaze as he nodded. "Do you need another set of hands?"

It still amazed her how different he was than any man she'd ever known. Women's work meant nothing to him.

She shook her head and squeezed his hand. "There's not much to do."

As she and Opal worked side by side at the sink, scrubbing the pots and rinsing them clean, there seemed to be a thickness in the air. Opal's normal peace was missing. That was apparent from both the tense set of her shoulders and the pinch of her mouth. Was she upset now that Tori planned to marry Ezra? Opal had almost pushed her that direction before, and she seemed to like Ezra well enough, but maybe seeing her younger cousin with a beau was too much even for Opal.

The knot pulled tighter in Tori's midsection. "Are you going to tell me what's bothering you or do I have to guess?"

Opal glanced sideways at her, and Tori met her gaze, but the flickering light from the lantern kept Opal's eyes shadowed. She looked back down to the pan she'd been scrubbing, and her hands resumed their work. "I've decided to take the job Ezra found for us in Mountain Bluff, with the Shumeisters." Opal's quiet tone was laced with enough resolve to make each word distinct, yet still, Tori must have heard her wrong.

"What are you talking about?" She gripped the edge of the counter. "We're staying here now. At the Rocky Ridge."

Opal looked up again, and this time Tori couldn't miss the shimmer in her gaze. "You're staying here, Tori. You have a wonderful man and a family who already love you. A home, everything you've always wanted. But I...I can't help but feel like something is waiting for me in Mountain Bluff. I was excited about the possibility there. Maybe I can make a difference, you know? At least to the

Shumeisters."

Tori grabbed Opal's wrist. "You are my family, Opal. You make a difference to me. To everyone you meet. I don't think I could stand it if you left me."

Opal twisted her arm so Tori's hand slid into hers, and she squeezed it. "I'm not leaving you, dear. We'll be just a couple days apart, and I'll come see you every Christmas. But I think you'll find you don't need me as much as you think you do. After all, you'll have a new husband and a new home to make your own. And you have the God you've been telling me about."

The burn of emotion clogged Tori's throat, creeping up to her eyes as she squeezed them shut and pulled Opal into a hug. "I'm not sure I can let you go."

Opal stroked her back, rubbing gentle circles. "I'm not going far. But I think this is what I need to do."

❧

*T*he next morning, Tori strolled along the riverbank in front of Mara's home, soaking in the warmth of the late morning sun. She and Opal had stayed up several hours the night before talking through their plans—mostly Opal's plans, really—and she was finally coming to grips with the idea.

A male voice called from across the river, and she spun at the familiar tenor. Her heart did a leap at the sight of man and horse splashing into the water, heading straight toward her.

"You finally came." She stood at the very edge of the bank, ready to meet his horse as the gelding reached the river's edge.

When they neared, Ezra gave her a cock-eyed grin. "Nice to see you, too."

That smile did funny things to her insides, but she kept talking so maybe he wouldn't see her blush. "I thought you might be here for breakfast."

He reined his horse to a halt when they reached dry ground, then dismounted and stepped close to Tori, slipping his arm around her waist. "I wanted to, but the telegraph was busy this morning."

His voice had slipped to a deeper vibrato, and his warm breath caressed her face. Almost intoxicating, being so close to this man.

She pressed her hand flat on his chest, fighting the urge to pull him closer, to tuck herself tightly against him, hiding inside his strength. Instead, she forced herself to give a teasing answer. "I suppose you should find a wife to help you with that."

She hazarded a quick glance at his face, but one look at the intensity in his gaze stole her courage.

"I suppose I should."

With her flat hand, she followed the line of the buttons parading down his shirt, then slipped sideways as her fingers found the beat of his heart. The pulse moved quicker than she'd expected.

"Tori."

"Hmm?"

He was quiet, so she forced herself to meet his gaze again. This time, his eyes had lost some of their heat, revealing an earnestness that made the longing in her chest pull even tighter.

She held his gaze, lost in the care she saw there, the love.

"Tori, Zeche asked if we wanted to go with them to South Pass—to be wed at the same time."

He paused, his gaze never wavering from hers. But the effect of his words set off a chain fire in her chest. Be married? Of course. But... weren't Zeche and Gretta planning to leave in just a few days? Could she do that? Marry Ezra in a week or less?

She studied him, fighting the current of emotions swirling inside her. She loved this man so much. If he wanted the wedding to take place that soon, she could do it. For him. She wanted to do it, she would just need to accustom herself to the idea. And spend a great deal of prayer to settle the remnants of fear that still churned in the bottom of her stomach.

Inhaling a steadying breath, she raised her chin and smiled into his eyes. "That sounds good."

He didn't answer right away, just held her gaze.

Through her eyes, she did her best to show him the love that had grown so quickly in her heart, that now flourished in every part of her. Could he see how happy he made her?

He raised his hand to cup her cheek. "I'm not so sure."

As the words reached her, their meaning settled over her almost like a slap. She blinked and pulled back. He didn't want her now? Had he finally come to his senses? Maybe Zeche didn't approve of her. But of course, he didn't. If Ezra had told him anything about her past, he wouldn't want his brother taking on a woman so stained.

But Ezra's arm stayed tight around her, not letting her go. "That's not what I mean, Tori. Nothing about my love for you has changed." With his free hand, he stroked her arm, starting at her shoulder and moving all the way down to her fingertips until she could scarcely draw breath from the power of his touch. "I love you too much to rush this. I want you to be ready. I want all traces of fear to be gone."

He pulled her closer, resting his forehead on hers. Their breaths mingled, forming a single cloud in the chilly air. "I'll wait as long as I need to." His lips were mere inches from hers, so close she already knew how his kiss would taste. "Besides, I think you need to be courted proper." Those lips—the corners tipped in the hint of a grin. "Like this."

That grin was the last thing she saw as her eyes sank shut and his mouth claimed hers. And with the sensation—the touch and taste of him—a sense of rightness settled over her stronger than anything she'd felt yet.

God had brought this man to her, a gift she'd never thought she was worthy of. Yet He'd proven His love, and continued to prove it with each wild beat of her heart.

Did you enjoy Ezra and Tori's story? I hope so!
Would you take a quick minute to leave a review?
It doesn't have to be long. Just a sentence or two telling what you liked about the story!

~

To receive a FREE short story and get updates when new Misty M. Beller books release, click here: mistymbeller.com/freebook

And here's a peek at the next book in the series, A Mountain
Christmas Romance (Opal's story!):

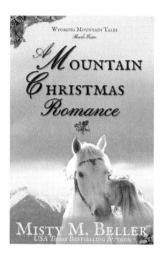

Chapter One

November 7, 1867
Mountain Bluff, Wyoming Territory

The thrill of speed pulsed through Matthias Bjork as he leaned low
over the horse's neck, the wind whipping the coarse white mane to his
face. He reined the gelding around a boulder, then wove through the
scattered pine and spruce trees. He knew from experience the creek
ahead would appear quickly once he rounded that cluster of cedars
just ahead.

The horse dodged right to skirt the evergreens, his muscles
bunching as he anticipated the coming leap over the water. The
animal loved adventure as much as Matthias, unafraid to grasp a thrill
wherever they found it.

The trees cleared, revealing the narrow chasm through which the
creek ran. He tightened his legs around the horse, lifting out of the
saddle to signal Karl into a jump.

But a flash of white underneath them caught his focus. A person?

The gelding had already begun his leap, and Matthias's shift in focus threw the animal off balance. As they soared over the gap between the banks, a squeal sounded beneath them, high pitched like that of a woman. Then a large splash. Had Karl's hooves struck her?

He didn't have time to wonder long, for his distraction had altered the momentum of the horse's jump. Karl's front hooves landed on the far shore, but as his rear hooves should have struck solid ground, the animal's back end seemed to scramble, then sink down as he fought for purchase.

Matthias leaned forward, trying to use his weight as an anchor to help the horse stay up on the bank. But Karl continued slipping, shifting backward as his hooves clattered against the rock surface of the four-foot cliff.

A scream sounded from behind, then the fury of splashing water. The horse was losing the battle to stay on the bank. Matthias kicked his boots free of the stirrups, scanning the area for the best place to jump. The chasm containing the stream wasn't more than four or five feet wide, so he would likely be dashed against the rocks on the far side if Karl fell backward.

He swung his leg over and pushed away to the left, trying to land on his feet in the water. His boots hit the icy stream with a splash, but the rocks littering the bottom threw off his balance, toppling him onto his side in the creek.

Cold.

Nay, freezing. The frigid liquid stole away his breath and nearly his senses.

But Karl's frantic thrashing helped restore the latter. Matthias scrambled away from the panicked horse who had also landed on his side, and was struggling to find footing in the small enclosure between the rock walls.

A figure moved on the other side of the horse. A woman standing in the creek bed, hand extended to the flailing animal. "Easy, boy. Don't struggle. Easy, there."

Her crooning seemed to work because Karl stilled. His heavy breathing filled the air as he lay in the water, sides heaving.

The woman approached, still murmuring. As she grabbed the reins, Matthias eased to his feet. Creek water dripped from him running down his left side that had been submerged. Numbness spread through his hands and feet, both from the wintery air and the water that was mostly run-off from snow higher in the mountains.

He ignored the bite of the cold and eased toward the horse as the woman attempted to maneuver him into a position that would make it easier to stand.

"When he tries to rise, pull him that way." Matthias motioned toward the left bank.

The woman looked up at him as though she'd just now noticed his presence, her eyes piercing with a crystal blue stare. His heart panged. With her blonde hair and delicate features, she looked much like his sister probably would now that she'd grown. And Alanna would be about this woman's age, or maybe a little older.

He studied her, but she turned away to urge the horse again. Still, he couldn't shake the power of the woman's presence. Could she be his long, lost sister? The only living family he had left? He'd been searching so long, finding her on this remote trail would be just like God's sense of humor.

Yet, a tiny part of him—the part of him that was all viral male— hoped that the beautiful creature helping to extricate his horse from the icy water was not a blood relation. In fact, her elfin features made it almost seem she might be a woodland nymph, like in the myths of old. The stories his parents had passed down from their Viking fore- fathers. Of course, the woodland nymphs were only legends, not flesh and blood like this damsel.

"Stand clear!"

Matthias leaped backward, jolting to the present as Karl gave a mighty lurch and scrambled to his feet, assisted by the woman's pull on his reins as she guided him to the only available space in the creek bed.

"Good, boy." She stepped forward to stroke the horse's neck as he stood heaving, water dripping from his winter coat where he'd lain in the stream.

Matthias moved to take the reins, trying to ignore his own wet clothing and the water sloshing in his boots. "I'll take him."

She handed over the leathers, but remained at Karl's neck, stroking the thick, wet hair and crooning.

Her nearness raised all the hairs along his arms, which were already gooquitefleshed from the chill of the icy water. He stepped back, away from Karl's head. Away from the woman.

He had to refocus on what needed done. "From whence do you hail?"

She glanced over at him, a curious light touching her crystal eyes. "Mountain Bluff. And you?"

"Nowhere." Twas his standard answer to that question. Nowhere. Many places. He'd wandered for so many years, he wasn't even sure what it would feel like to belong in a place.

She raised her fair brows, which were almost exactly the varying strains of fresh honey. But at the moment, the perfect arch of those brows clearly communicated her wary frustration with his answer.

"Nowhere, sir?" If he'd not caught the message portrayed by her expression, the exasperation dripping from her tone said it even better.

He shrugged. "I hail from these mountains. What are you doing so far from town?" This spot must be at least an hour's trek on foot.

"Gathering herbs."

Now it was his turn to raise his brows. "In winter?"

She studied him, as though taking his measure. "Yes. My apologies for startling your horse." She turned back to Karl and offered him a final pat, then stepped back.

As she moved away, Matthias gathered both the animal and his wits. "Are you here alone, then? Your husband allowed you to wander so far unescorted?"

"I have no husband. I work for a family there, and as I said, I'm gathering herbs to replenish our supplies."

As she spoke, she scooped up a basket he hadn't noticed on the ground, then rummaged through it. Not sparing him a single glance.

But her words pricked Matthias's memory. The last time he'd

stopped at Mountain Bluff, Vatti Shumeister had mentioned the woman they hired to help Mutti Shumeister with her baking. The lady had been away visiting relatives at the time, but...could this fair-haired nymph be her? He'd pictured a plain-faced spinster, too vinegarish to find a husband, even in this land crawling with eager bachelors.

He eyed her. "Do you work for the Shumeisters?"

She jerked her head up, finally giving him notice. "You know them?"

He nodded. Yes, Vatti and Mutti Shumeister were the closest to family he'd had for years. Other than his sister, of course. Which was why he had to find her.

He turned back to Karl. "I'll need to lead him downstream to a place where the bank is not as steep. Then we'll take you home." If she belonged to the Shumeisters, she had now become his responsibility. And he certainly wasn't going to leave her alone and on foot so far from town.

He found a place about thirty yards downstream, and Karl seemed as eager as he was to escape the icy water. But as they trudged back on dry ground, the water squished in his soggy boots. It would be a long ride to Mountain Bluff.

The woman knelt over her basket when he and Karl reached her side.

He vaulted into the saddle, then extended his hand. "Give me your basket first, then I'll help you climb up."

She spared him a glance, and the disdain emanating from her look made it clear she didn't plan to accept his offer. "I'll return on my own when I'm ready."

He didn't lower his hand. "I can't leave you out here. Haven't you gathered all the herbs you need?" What could she possibly find in this season, with all the plants barren of leaves?

She didn't answer, just straightened to her feet and started walking away.

Exasperation simmered in his gut. What was wrong with this woman?

He nudged Karl forward to follow her, then reined in when they came abreast of her. "Miss. I'm not leaving you out here. If there's something more to gather, tell me and I'll help. Or I can even come back for it." That would be the more pleasant option, given the fact that his toes had already benumbed and his boots had stiffened as though developing a shell of ice.

"I don't mean to cause you trouble, sir." She didn't give him a moment's notice with the words.

He let out a huff. "You're causing me more trouble by refusing than if you'd just hand me the basket and climb on the horse. Not to mention you may have the power to save my damp feet from frostbite if you make haste."

She turned a startled gaze on him, studying his face first, then lowering to his boots. Her shoulders slumped as though she'd eased out a sigh, and she handed the basket up to him.

When his hand touched her cold one, a warmth spread up his arm, washing all the way through him to his toes. She seemed to be experienced with horses as she fit her boot into the stirrup and swung up behind him.

He gave her a moment to settle, then nudged Karl forward. Twas harder than he'd expected to ignore the warmth of her behind him, even though she sat with a gap of several inches between them.

She didn't speak, and he allowed an easy silence to settle, enough for him to mull over a few things that had struck him as odd. "It seems like you've ridden a horse before."

He waited. She didn't speak, so he waited longer.

Finally, she said, "Yes."

That was all? He hadn't asked a direct question, but her response was more than short.

"Did you learn to ride after you came to Mountain Bluff?"

"No." At least this time, her answer was more forthcoming, although edging even closer to rude.

But her curt response gave him the impetus to push farther. "Where did you live before coming to this place?"

"My cousin and I came from Pennsylvania." Her voice softened this time, coming out almost meek. And something about the tone sent of pang to his chest.

"Is that where you learn to ride? In Pennsylvania?"

"Yes."

Again with the one-word answers. But she still had that melancholy tone that made him want to cease his inquisition.

Once more the silence settled, and he tried to find his easy rhythm. The peace that always came on the trail, riding through the scrawny pines with rocky peaks rising all around him.

But the calm in his spirit seemed elusive this time. Maybe twas his body so stirred from the nearness of such a lovely woman. Or maybe twas the fact he couldn't seem to draw her into conversation. Not that he was terribly experienced with women. In fact, he rarely interacted with the fairer gender except for the occasional boardinghouse matron or cafeteria serving girl, and he didn't usually give half a moment's consideration to what they thought of him. But something about this woman made him crave her good opinion.

Or maybe, he just wanted to hear that smile in her voice, the one that lit her features when she'd stroked his horse.

"Have you ever owned a horse, Miss...?" He searched his mind for her surname. Had Mutti or Vatti ever mentioned it? She didn't fill in the gap, so it seemed he'd have to ask outright. "What *is* your name?"

"Miss Opal Boyd."

He took in a breath for patience, then let it out. "Have you ever owned a horse, Miss Boyd?" It seemed she would make him force every syllable she would deign to offer.

"Yes, Mr. Björk."

He looked over his shoulder to study her. "How do you know my name?"

She shrugged. "I assumed that's who you were. You didn't introduce yourself, but the Shumeisters speak of you often."

He couldn't help the warmth that flowed through his chest. Not only did they think of him when he wasn't there, but they even mentioned him. But he only allowed a small nod as he turned back to the trail.

After another quarter hour, the silence had officially stretched his nerves taught. The land leveled out, opening to a wide valley and open trail. This particular open area spread for almost a mile. The perfect landscape to pull Miss Opal Boyd from her reserve.

Perhaps. It might be worth the effort.

"You should probably hold on tighter for this stretch of land."

Her body stiffened behind him. "Why?"

"It would just be a good idea." Let her shake loose a bit if she didn't want to take his advice. They'd start slowly enough that he could make sure she didn't actually slide off Karl's back. But just in case... "Actually, you might do best to hold around my waist."

The noise in his ear sounded like a snort, not something that would escape the mouth of a woodland nymph.

He bit back a smile as he pressed a heel into Karl's side.

The gelding pushed into a canter, and her snort was replaced with a squeal. He reached to grab her coat so she didn't slide off. At almost the same moment, she gripped the sides of his own coat, jerking him back with the momentum of the horse's speed. He reached for the horn and was barely able to keep them both on the horse's back.

Karl never slowed through it all, and when they'd both regained their balance, Matthias crouched low and gave the horse his head. Miss Boyd had finally taken his advice and now clutched tightly around his waist.

The wind whipped at them, bringing an icy chill that made all his senses spring to life. The horse's white mane flapped in his face, raising up the scent of the wild that always centered him. His mouth found its usual grin, possibly heightened by the pretty woman clinging to him.

Too soon, the end of the valley loomed ahead and he straightened, easing back on Karl's reins. Behind him, Miss Boyd leaned away from him, although she didn't release her clutch around his middle.

When Karl settled back to a walk, he turned to glimpse her. Would she be angry? She'd been hard to read at times, so maybe she was one of those uptight schoolmarms who didn't know how to enjoy a carefree moment.

When he turned, she was tucked so tight against him, it was hard to catch more than a glimpse of her grin. She noticed him looking and eased back, not quite meeting his eye. The way she had her lower lip tucked in her teeth didn't hide her smile, though. Not when a twinkle lit her crystal blue eyes.

And that twinkle did funny things in his chest. Stirring up a sensation he'd do best to shun.

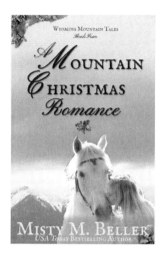

Get A Mountain Christmas Romance at your favorite retailer.

ABOUT THE AUTHOR

 **Misty M. Beller** is a *USA Today* bestselling author of romantic mountain stories, set on the 1800s frontier and woven with the truth of God's love.

Raised on a farm and surrounded by family, Misty developed her love for horses, history, and adventure. These days, her husband and children provide fresh adventure every day, keeping her both grounded and crazy.

Misty's passion is to create inspiring Christian fiction infused with the grandeur of the mountains, writing historical romance that displays God's abundant love through the twists and turns in the lives of her characters.

Sharing her stories with readers is a dream come true for Misty. She writes from her country home in South Carolina and escapes to the mountains any chance she gets.

Connect with Misty at www.MistyMBeller.com

ALSO BY MISTY M. BELLER

Call of the Rockies

Freedom in the Mountain Wind

Hope in the Mountain River

Light in the Mountain Sky

Courage in the Mountain Wilderness

Faith in the Mountain Valley

Honor in the Mountain Refuge

Peace in the Mountain Haven

Grace on the Mountain Trail

Calm in the Mountain Storm

Brides of Laurent

A Warrior's Heart

A Healer's Promise

A Daughter's Courage

Hearts of Montana

Hope's Highest Mountain

Love's Mountain Quest

Faith's Mountain Home

Texas Rancher Trilogy

The Rancher Takes a Cook

The Ranger Takes a Bride

The Rancher Takes a Cowgirl

Wyoming Mountain Tales

A Pony Express Romance

A Rocky Mountain Romance

A Sweetwater River Romance

A Mountain Christmas Romance

The Mountain Series

The Lady and the Mountain Man

The Lady and the Mountain Doctor

The Lady and the Mountain Fire

The Lady and the Mountain Promise

The Lady and the Mountain Call

This Treacherous Journey

This Wilderness Journey

This Freedom Journey (novella)

This Courageous Journey

This Homeward Journey

This Daring Journey

This Healing Journey

Made in United States
North Haven, CT
23 February 2023

33066313R00121